ETERNAL VIGILANCE

The Divided America Zombie Apocalypse

Book Four

B. D. Lutz

ACKNOWLEDGEMENTS

Edited by Monique Happy Editorial Services
www.moniquehappyeditorial.com

Thank you for your hard work and guidance. But most of all, thank you for answering a random email from a newbie.

Cover designed by: Kelly A. Martin
www.kam.design

Kelly, you are a master at your craft!

Photography by lchumpitaz (DepositPhotos), olga_simonova_ph (DepositPhotos), benkrut(DepositPhotos), gsagi (DepositPhotos), Leoq (DepositPhotos), nilovsergei (DepositPhotos), YAYImages (DepositPhotos), realinemedia (DepositPhotos), chagpg (DepositPhotos)

PROLOGUE

October 30th, 2018
One Week Prior To The Divide

Shafter glared across the conference table at the freshman congresswoman from New York. She'd been a disrupter from day one, and today was no exception. She interjected with nonsensical observations and utterly ridiculous strategies at every stage of the conversation. Her manner of speaking was like nails on a chalkboard. *When did public schools stop teaching proper pronunciation?*

At his wits' end, Shafter moved to muzzle the Pit Bull once and for all. "Representative Cortina. We are one week away from the people of our great nation voting to divide into two separate countries. I'm advising you that the time for your useless ramblings has passed. Our plan is already in play. Our poll numbers are strong. We will prevail. So please stop speaking."

Cortina's mouth snapped shut. She was stunned by the harsh rebuke from her colleague, but only for the briefest of moments. She pulled a sharp breath and plowed forward with her statement, "As I was saying before the most esteemed Senator Shafter interjected. Our reliance upon polling in 2016 is what led us to this point." She locked Shafter with an icy stare and continued, "The stakes are, like, much higher this time. We must apply more pressure. And apply it non-stop until we count every single vote."

Shafter slammed his notepad to the table. His patience had vanished. It was his turn to talk. "We have submerged this country in violent protests for two years. TWO YEARS.

During that time, our staffs have fed a never-ending stream of misinformation to the media. We have infiltrated every college campus in the country. Ms. Cortina, simply put, we've inflicted the damage necessary to succeed in turning this entire country to our party."

Cortina gazed defiantly over the rims of her unnecessary eyeglasses. The political vipers seated across the table from her had become irrelevant. She would act on her own, but first they needed to suffer her anger. "Speaker Piles, Senator Shafter, Congressman Shank, and Senator Finkelstein. You are making a mistake. Like, one that will cost us dearly. You are short-sighted, withered prunes. Bottom feeders, actually. I will act to ensure we win this vote. When I'm elected President of our newly established country, I will have each of you tried for, like, treason or something."

Piles' incensed expression belied her evenly toned response to the child seated across the table from her. She locked the freshman in an icy stare and slurred her response, "Dear, bless your heart, where did you attend college? I can barely understand you when you, LIKE, speak." Waving a liver-spotted hand in dismissal, she continued, "Never mind. It's not important. And knowing who's responsible for your education won't change the fact that you're an idiot."

Cortina bristled, hinging her oversized maw open to respond, but Piles stepped on her words. "You will do as you're told. Have I been clear?"

Cortina shot to her feet and stormed from the room. She would take the appropriate action to ensure they won. No longer did she need the irrelevant politicians of yesteryear. She was "New and Now," with fresh ideas and a mind free from the bourbon-soaked delusions of has-beens.

Her footfalls echoed loudly in the hallowed halls of the Capitol Building as she stormed back to her private office. Her administrative assistant startled when the door burst open and slammed against the wall. She stood and approached the petulant child across the visitor's waiting area. Cortina waved her off, then screamed, "I need cold, filtered, un-bottled water. Are you capable of that task, Betty?"

Her assistant had grown used to Cortina's demeaning ways. She wrote it off to poor interpersonal skills that so many of her generation suffered from. She still disliked the young woman but needed the health insurance afforded by her position. With that thought in mind, she spun on her heel and proceeded to the cafeteria where she kept Cortina's supply of water. She smirked at the thought that she'd been bringing the brat bottled water, poured into a pitcher, since the day the witch set foot in the office. *It's the little things,* she mused as she sauntered towards the cafeteria.

Waiting a ten-count after Betty's exit, Cortina pressed the send button on her personal cell. After two rings, a thick Hungarian accent filled the speaker. Not waiting for salutations, she launched into the conversation. "We need more protesters in the streets by day's end. Advise on their locations and I'll inform my contacts where to send their news crews."

CHAPTER 1 – SCALE

Shafter's swollen eyes glared at Williams. "Is that what you wanted to hear? IS IT? We're responsible for everything, the violence, The Divide, the virus. All of it." Spittle flew from the senator's mouth as he screamed, "I... *we* are the reason the world is dying. But you have to believe me, this was not our intent. We wanted to reunite the country."

Williams leaned into the dim light thrown by the room's single overhead light bulb, casting his face in demonic shadows. "I always suspected you had your thumb on the scale. But you were standing on it. You tore us apart." He glared at the senator, reveling in his fear. "Now I tear you apart." He turned his head towards the door. "Guard, did you get what you needed?"

A single knock came in response. Shafter's eyes bulged. "What's the meaning of this? That's entrapment. You cannot use my words against me in court."

Williams stood, a wicked grin dominating his features as he stalked towards the senator. "Shafter, *this* was your trial. You're guilty as charged. Now we move to the punishment phase of our proceedings."

The guard waited until Shafter's screams ceased, then knocked twice. Williams stood facing the door, the senator's broken body at his feet, and told the guard to enter. He was ready for this to end.

A smile creased his face as the executioner entered the room.

CHAPTER 2 – GHOST

Nathan smashed Ghost through the skull of the monster which bore a striking resemblance to Elvis. The resulting explosion hurled gore in every direction. The now headless body tumbled down the rocky hillside, splashing into the water below. Twirling Ghost in his right hand, Nathan prepared to annihilate the last of the undead freaks. With the force of ten men, he swung for the fences, finding the monster's neck. The sound of shattering vertebrae and skin tearing spurred his rage. He pulled Ghost back and used the end of her barrel like a pool cue, sending the beast to rest on the unforgiving rocks jutting from the hillside.

Nathan bent, hands on knees, gasping for air while allowing the bloodlust to clear from his mind. He stared at the lifeless husks strewn about the ragged rocks below, their devastated bodies a testament to the brutality of his assault.

The blood of his victims dripped from the barrel of his Easton Ghost baseball bat. Its thirty-three inches extended his kill zone, enabling him to dispatch the monsters before they crept close enough to latch onto him. He'd seen it repeatedly. People underestimated these devils only to get pulled apart and devoured.

He rose to his full six feet and screamed, "This hill belongs to me! Have I made myself clear? I was homeless, not helpless." His voice echoed through the derelict buildings surrounding his hill.

Something inside him had sparked to life when he'd left his home two weeks earlier. The violence felt familiar to him.

5

It calmed and focused him. His movements were precise, each battle playing in his mind's eye before he swung Ghost. Yes, he was built for this, built for violence.

Nathan retreated into the copse of exotic foliage that had served as his home for the last two days. It afforded him an elevated view of his surroundings while the water encircling it functioned as an early warning system. His position also enabled him to observe the Blue States United soldiers as they corralled the monsters into trucks and whisked them away.

Initially he'd thought BSU had finally mounted a counterstrike, but that logic didn't fit. Why not kill them? Risking human life to load them up for termination at some remote location wasn't how you fought a war. He didn't understand why he recognized the flaw in their tactics, but he did.

He curled into a ball as the evening air chilled. The climate reminded him of a place he had visited, a land with sweltering days and cool nights, fraught with danger. Nathan realized he had to leave this place. He needed food, a fortified shelter, and a bed to make. That simple task started each of his days; it centered him, gave him a slight sense of pride.

The last day he'd made his bed was the day he'd overheard the conversation between Wild Bill and that North Korean agent. Nathan had noticed the duo of DPRK operatives lurking around the Sepulveda Basin encampment weeks earlier and avoided them like the plague. The drugs they peddled to the encampment's residents were potent and shielded the DPRK operatives from the abrasive reception usually shown to newcomers to the Sepulveda Basin.

He'd told the police about the Asian dope-slingers but couldn't articulate how he knew they were DPRK agents. *I just do* wasn't good enough for LA's finest.

Nathan didn't understand why the conversation between Wild and the DPRK agent had set his mind on fire, but he'd known it was time to abandon his tin shack and leave Los Angeles. He was driven east by an invisible force to seek safety behind Right America's walls.

By the time he'd reached the Nevada border, he was killing dozens of monsters every day. The fighting never ended. His blistered hands screamed at him to stop as he wielded sticks and rocks, fighting for his life.

He could have cried with joy when he stumbled across the deserted baseball diamonds just off I-15 in Hesperia. That's where he'd found Ghost lying forgotten among the rotting corpses.

The low rumble of a diesel engine broke his thoughts. Nathan's mind sputtered like a TV trying to tune in a channel, then went crystal clear. He needed to know what the BSU soldiers were doing with the dead.

The transport came into view a moment after clarity struck him. Nathan gathered his meager possessions into his backpack and waited for his opportunity. The tractor-trailer backed up to the enormous doors of the glitzy glass and concrete building. Regardless of the building's marquee, this was no mirage.

Twenty feet before the entrance, a soldier exited the cab, opened the doors of the trailer, and directed the driver into position between the barriers set up as a funnel for the dead. When the truck stopped, a second soldier exited and took a position opposite the first. With a nod, they both grasped a large steel pole attached to the building's doors and pulled. As the doors inched open, the dead exited one by one.

From his vantage point, Nathan watched countless dead fighting against the building's glass entrance, trying to escape. *If the glass fails, the monsters will pour into the streets.* He'd no sooner finished the thought when he heard it. The telltale sound of glass failing!

Both soldiers dropped their poles and bolted for the truck's cab, abandoning the monsters already headed for its trailer. *NOW!* his mind screamed, and he broke from cover, focused on the truck's empty spare tire carrier mounted beneath the trailer. The truck bucked and kicked as the panicked driver tried to find a gear, giving Nathan the time needed to catch up to the rig and calculate how he would stuff his sizeable frame into the compact space.

The sound of glass shattering spurred him to action. He grabbed the underside of the moving trailer and slid in legs first. When his groin slammed into the center support beam, the pain nearly rendered him unconscious. He lost his grip on the trailer and his upper body arched backward, leaving his head mere inches from the pavement rushing by. Fighting through the pain, he first righted his upper body then began folding himself into the tight space. He repositioned his legs to one side and scooted his upper body out of sight. Nathan brought Ghost to his chest and fed her through his backpack's chest straps. Her cool aluminum body calmed him.

Staring up at the corrugated metal as the pavement rushed by beneath him, he realized he was smiling. His pulse quickened as he grasped the reality that had eluded him for years. He was doing what he was meant to do. *I'm a soldier!*

As the truck rolled on, Nathan's body paid the price for his poor choice of concealment. During the hours' long journey, the truck rumbled over dead bodies, chuckholes, and curbs, slamming him around his metal confines. The impacts promised to snap his spine and probably would have if not for the small amount of cushioning his backpack provided. He had lost the feeling in his dangling legs, and Ghost managed to bust his lip after a particularly hard jolt.

He was searching for a way to support his back and legs when the semi made a hard left turn, nearly ejecting him to the road to be crushed under the big-rig's rear wheels. After some maneuvering, the truck inched backwards, then came to an abrupt stop.

He readied himself when the cab doors slammed, followed by the footfalls of its occupants.

"Why's the truck empty?" a voice yelled over the idling engine.

A screeching voice answered, "We damn near got eaten alive, that's why."

Another voice chimed in, "This is bullshit. No more trips to Vegas, or anyplace else for that matter. We've dumped thousands of these monsters. I'm done. And when the hell are we getting a resupply? When is BSU…"

A gunshot silenced the voice. When Nathan saw a lifeless body slam to the dusty ground, he knew it was time to move.

He eased himself out of hiding. With his legs still numb, he crawled to some nearby brush and faded into the landscape.

In a growling whisper he made a promise, "I will end this place."

CHAPTER 3 – BEAUTIFUL SOUND

As the sun faded into the horizon, Nathan emerged from the cluster of brittle bush and yucca he had been hiding behind. His mind no longer struggled to find his memories. He was a soldier and today he would join the fight to win back his country.

Nathan crept to the side of the building housing the big-rigs and their drivers. Removing Ghost from his backpack, he approached the open overhead garage doors. Four BSU soldiers huddled around a tiny folding table, playing poker at the edge of the opening. Money was won and lost while the men hurled insults at each other's mothers, sisters, and girlfriends.

He considered the banter and realized he'd be facing young, capable men. His attack would need to be swift and merciless. Nathan's only advantage was the element of surprise.

As he leaned his head around the corner of the building, a soldier suddenly lurched across the table, sending cash and playing cards skittering across the floor. "You cheating scumbag!" he hollered at an unseen player.

The area erupted with the sound of angry men trying to beat one another to death. The timing was perfect. Nathan charged the area and brought Ghost across the face of the first soldier he encountered. The sound of bones fracturing resonated over the din of battle, drawing the attention of a soldier who had avoided the brawl and was frantically grabbing the cash strewn about the floor.

He locked eyes with Nathan as Ghost began her deadly descent towards his head. His reluctance to drop the cash clutched in his fists cost him his life. His face split open as Ghost crushed his skull.

Nathan spun toward the two remaining soldiers locked in a life or death struggle on the oil-stained concrete. He reared back and sent Ghost whistling through the air. With no specific target, he let Ghost choose her victim. Nathan feared she would overshoot the men when the brawl's agitator suddenly gained the upper hand and climbed atop his opponent. As he prepared to pummel the double dealer, he glanced up to find Ghost inches from his face.

Her sleek form found his forehead and destroyed his cranium; the impact sent blood streaming down his shirt as his lifeless body slammed to the unforgiving concrete.

Nathan rushed to secure the soldiers and retrieve his weapon. He checked the pulse of Ghost's latest victim and found none. He knelt next to the only living soldier, whose dazed expression gave way to fear as Nathan's wild face filled his vision. He grabbed the soldier by the neck and whispered, "You can show me where you're taking the dead, or you can die. The choice is yours."

Forty-six minutes later, Nathan stood on a ridge overlooking RAM's border wall between Nevada and Utah. Nature stretched out before him in a stunning display of her raw beauty.

With the dead soldier at his feet and hundreds of undead monsters roaming the border wall, he raged at what the world had become. He watched the monsters as they forced themselves through a human-sized breach in the wall and entered the rugged terrain of Dixie National Forest.

Speaking only to the cool breeze blowing through his mangy hair, Nathan said, "This is the perfect place to infiltrate your enemy: isolated, unforgiving, and unguarded." He began forming a plan to plug the breach and end the flow of death into RAM. The plan included him living through whatever actions he took. He had someone he needed to see again, and these monsters would not stop him!

Nathan took his first step just as the beautiful sound reached his ears.

CHAPTER 4 – WHERE I BELONG

"Wicked One for Wicked Three, how copy?"

"Go for Wicked Three, over."

"Break formation and put eyes on the smoke west of our target. Report findings. Engage hostiles, over."

"Wicked Three, breaking formation, out."

Chief Warrant Officer Jennings watched through her port glass as Wicked Three broke formation and sped towards the smoke billowing on the horizon. If they had a wildfire to contain while fighting the apocalypse, Jennings worried it would be the proverbial straw that broke their backs.

After two in-flight refuels and joining up with five A10 Warthogs over Hill AFB, they were finally approaching their target. The crew's anticipation had morphed into anxiety, highlighted by the lack of radio chatter. Three of the four Black Hawk helos under her command held six combat-hardened soldiers. The fourth held the equipment needed to plug the breach.

The mission objective mandated boots on the ground to seal the breach after the area was scrubbed by the A10s and Black Hawk M134 Miniguns. With the heavy ground cover and rugged terrain, it would be a best guess that the area was clear enough to put their war fighters on the ground. None of them liked the plan.

"Wicked Three for Wicked One, how copy?"

Jennings still had Wicked Three in sight, and it hadn't reached its target. Something was happening. "Go for Wicked One."

"Chief, I have eyes on a living person."

Jennings felt a rush of panic. "Engage the target. We don't have time to play with BSU soldiers."

"Chief, the person is waving to get our attention. He's wearing RAM ACUs. Requesting permission to investigate?"

Jennings didn't like it, but the information about the ACUs needed further investigation. They didn't leave their own behind. "Recon the area for threats. Fast rope two. Keep your gun on the target. Eliminate if needed."

"Roger that, Wicked Three, out."

Jennings pulled her Hawk to a hover a quarter mile from the target and let the A10s take the lead. Less than five minutes later, their GAU-8, 30mm Gatling guns roared to life.

The telltale purr of the devastating weapon brought a smile to her face. She realized the low-n-slow attack runs the heavily armored warbirds specialized in made them the perfect choice for this mission. *Please don't hit that wall,* Jennings thought as the Warthogs began their runs.

The A10s formed up single file, descending one at a time on their target. Plumes of earth exploded from the landscape, tossing shattered trees skyward and decimating the once-beautiful forest. The last Warthog in the formation released a five-hundred-pound MK-82 low-drag bomb on each run.

The Hogs made three runs on the area located inside the RAM-controlled side of the wall, creating a roughly one-hundred-yard wreckage-filled clearing for the soldiers to work in. When they pulled off and settled into an overwatch flight pattern, her Hawks took over. After a slow pass along the wall, they located the exact location of the breach. Time to go to work!

She gave a command, bringing the Hawks M134s online. The door-gunners concentrated their fire on the perimeter of the clearing created by the A10s. Any UCs shambling inside the dense foliage were surely dead now.

Jennings scanned the debris field. Nothing moved. The devastation was complete. Satisfied with what she saw, she barked into her coms, "We have a clear IP (insertion point). Deploy when ready. Wicked Four, drop your cargo, then reposition to provide covering fire on the BSU side of the wall."

Within seconds, the soldiers hit the ground, setting up a defensive perimeter. They waited until Wicked Four was in position, then approached the breach. Moments later, the Sappers engaged the portable gas welder, sending sparks flying as they secured the breach.

"Wicked One for Wicked Three, how copy?"

"Wicked One, this is Wicked Three, good copy."

"I need a SITREP, Wicked Three. We need your team on the ground."

"Wicked Three is en route. We secured one survivor on board. Jennings, you're not going to believe it."

Jennings powered down her Black Hawk and bolted from the cab. Wicked Three had just touched down, but she couldn't wait. The survivor inside of Wicked Three required her full attention. She had to see him.

Sergeant Major McMaster soon joined her. His obvious anticipation echoed hers. Their eyes met in a disbelieving stare, prompting her to move in and embrace the lifelong military man. His crusty veneer melted as he gripped her tight in his arms.

As soon as the cabin door retracted, the two rushed the Hawk. None of the soldiers in the cabin tried to exit. After an agonizing thirty seconds, a scruffy, grime-covered man emerged. McMaster went weak at the knees. Through the matted hair and long beard he saw his son's eyes!

McMaster rushed to his son, the son he thought he'd lost forever. He tried to talk, to will the words from his mouth, but couldn't. He gripped the sides of his boy's face tight and pulled him close. Resting his forehead to Nathan's, he sobbed. His only child was alive!

Kathy Jennings joined the men and wrapped her arms around them. Her childhood sweetheart, her best friend, was home. Her surrogate family was complete again.

***

Neon-green fingernails dropped trash into the garbage bag tied to her waist. From her position at the intersection of Henry Drive and Marshall Drive, she was afforded an unobstructed view of the scene unfolding on Marshall Army Airfield. She stopped working to witness the powerful sergeant major embrace another man.

His posture told her that his emotions were barely in control, and she thought she saw his knees buckle ever so slightly.

A seed was sown.

***

Two hours later, Sergeant Major McMaster sat staring at his son. Nathan was now clean-shaven and fed, wearing crisp ACUs.

He smiled at his father and asked, "What's on your mind? Never mind, I already know, and I don't blame you. Blue States United gave no warning before they emptied the military hospitals. They tossed us into the streets, Dad. I had no memory of my past, where I should go. Hell, I didn't even remember I had a father waiting for me."

The elder McMaster blinked slowly. He was reliving the countless searches he'd conducted for his son and the soldiers like him. BSU had cast them to the street like trash. Never attempted to contact family or even RAM military leaders. Dozens of them were found living in homeless encampments. They'd arrived too late to save others who became so desperate that they took their own lives. Reminding himself that Nathan was safe now, he tamped down his anger. But he promised himself a pound of flesh.

"Nathan, I'm sorry for what they put you through. But mostly, I'm sorry that I didn't find you. I searched for you every chance I had. When the virus hit… well, you know… Get some sleep, son. We have some catching up to do."

"I know you did, Dad. And sleep sounds good; sleeping in a proper bed sounds like heaven."

His dad choked up at his words, so Nathan quickly shifted gears. "Dad, I'm going to start training tomorrow. When it was time to fight, my training brought me back, brought my mind back. Dad, I'm where I belong."

CHAPTER 5 – UNDERSTANDING

Willis stood in front of Sergeant Major McMaster's desk. The cramped space felt barely large enough to display the man's citations and medals. Willis, not easily impressed, found himself overcome with admiration for his new CO.

It became clear that McMaster had regularly put himself in harm's way for his country. This man was a soldier's soldier, and Willis recognized he could learn a great deal from him.

McMaster glanced up from the manila folder and locked eyes with Willis. "I'm reading your file, but you're already aware of that." He seemed aggravated, and Willis questioned what exactly his file held that would cause the reaction.

"You're correct, Sergeant Major."

McMaster placed the folder on his desk and said, "Sergeant Willis, why the hell are you here? Your file tells me you should be back at Hopkins leading your men into battle."

Willis' perplexed stare prompted McMaster to continue, "You'll understand my question when I tell you what your new assignment is."

Willis grew uneasy, and, sensing this, McMaster asked him to sit. Steepling his fingers, he told Willis, "You have been assigned to the Vice President's daughter. I don't have the security clearance required to know the scope of your assignment. But I can guarantee you it is not important enough to remove you from the battlefield." He paused while his eyes clouded with painful memories, then continued, "You remind me of my son. Like you, he is a warrior. It came naturally to him. I know how he would react under these circumstances. Therefore, I will refuse to take corrective action if you are, shall we say, less than accommodating in your assignment."

Unsure how to respond, Willis simply asked where he should report. McMaster smiled and held the papers out. When Willis tried to take them from him, the sergeant major held them tight. Willis gave McMaster a questioning stare, to which he responded, "I'm going to work on your transfer back to Hopkins this afternoon. RAM needs your boots on the ground." He nodded, released the paperwork, and dismissed Willis.

The young soldier stood and, with a brisk salute, exited the office. His gut clenched as he reviewed the base map hanging in the Command Center's lobby. He would report to a home in an area labeled "VIP Housing Units." The housing area was highlighted in neon-yellow and appeared to have been established after the virus' outbreak. Speaking to no one in particular, he asked, "How many soldiers' families got displaced for this group of idiots."

He flinched when a voice said, "Twenty."

Willis spun around and said, "I'm sorry... I don't understand?"

"You asked how many families were displaced to establish the VIP housing units. The answer is twenty."

Willis regarded the young administrative specialist seated behind her desk in the Command Center's lobby. She hadn't been at her station when he'd arrived with McMaster. He would have remembered the attractive woman.

"You must be Sergeant Willis. I received a message for you from Camp Hopkins." Her apprehensive stare telegraphed that he was about to receive bad news.

Willis found himself in the street outside the Command Center. His world tilted hard to the right as he fought a losing battle against gravity. His right knee slammed to the ground, and he stitched his eyes shut, trying to steady his mind.

His family's home was under attack, and he found himself a thousand miles away. Helpless!

He caught movement when he opened his eyes. A teenage girl was quickly approaching.

**

Andrea didn't know why, but it was clear that she needed to help the war-fighter kneeling in the street. She had witnessed him stumble from the Command Center and struggle to remain standing.

When he lost his fight, something in her soul demanded that she act. That she help the men and women risking their lives to save the world. The same ones that'd risked their lives to rescue her.

The image of the soldier on bent knee coupled with what she'd witnessed four days ago when McMaster reunited with the man she later learned was his son—a son whom her country had treated like garbage—drove her forward.

Shame crept into her mind as she recalled how she and the other survivors had treated them. It was an emotion unfamiliar to her. It replaced her victim mentality and her distain for RAM's military. It was time to give back to the soldiers fighting to save her worthless hide.

**

Willis caught a flash of neon-green and quickly determined that a confrontation was coming in his direction. When the visitor's badge strung around her neck came into view, it removed all doubt. She was going to "protest" him.

His left knee found the pavement with a loud clack from the hard plastic knee protection. He hinged up to meet her stare and said, "Please, just stay away from me. I don't have the energy to stop myself from killing you."

Understanding swept through her. *He thinks I'm going to go full anarchist on him.* She smiled and said, "I don't blame you for thinking or saying that. Not long ago, you would have been right. But actually, I just want to thank you. I'm sorry for whatever happened to bring a man, excuse me, a war-fighter like you to his knees. I know any words I'd offer would only ring hollow. So please accept my thanks. I'm grateful for you and the men and women you serve with."

Andrea offered him her hand. "Get on your feet, soldier. The world is depending on you."

Stunned to silence, Willis accepted her help. When it became clear that he was steady, she turned on her heel and rushed away. For the first time in her life, she wasn't furious that she hadn't received praise for something she'd done.

She stormed across the base, her way made clear by McMaster's forced marches. Blasting into the Command Center and past a shocked Administrative Specialist, fearful of losing her nerve, she rushed into McMaster's office.

The man that had planted this seed, the one growing deep roots in her soul, slid a hand down his face in frustration. When his mouth hinged open, she stepped on his words. "Sergeant Major McMaster, it's time I became a part of something that matters. Something bigger than my tiny, hate-filled world. I want to enlist."

Chapter 6 – Chubby

The C130s, call signs Chubby One and Chubby Two from the 179th Air Lift Wing out of Mansfield, Ohio, prepared to leave RAM's airspace. The mission target, Alameda Island, lay less than an hour away.

Chubby One, piloted by Warrant Officers Dan Rite and copilot Silvia Brent, had been struggling to bring the starboard sprayers back online. They were green lights for most of the flight but went red on them an hour ago. The flight engineer had been fighting with the hastily assembled spray system ever since. The system mimicked a crop-duster's mechanism ramped up on a gargantuan scale.

"Ortiz, what's the status on the sprayers?" Brent asked over the in-flight radio.

"Status remains nonfunctioning. I've traced the lines back to the serum bladder, and they're clear. No blockages or kinks. The portal feeding the wing-mounted sprayers is inaccessible. Also, working in this wretched hazmat suit isn't helping my mood or maneuverability."

Brent chuckled at Ortiz's crusty response. "Keep at it. If they remain inoperable, we'll make it work using the port-side system."

The last-minute addition of the hazmat suits put them on edge. They were donned only by the flight crew members coming in direct contact with the bladders. But it still worried the entire team. They'd also lost a crewmember after they performed preflight blood tests, also outside of normal operating procedures. Rite received no explanation, just that their loadmaster wouldn't be joining them.

"This is Chubby One for Chubby Two, how copy?"

"Chubby Two, good copy."

"Fontana, our starboard sprayer remains offline. We'll be forced to make additional runs. How's your fuel? Over.

"Fuel is a go. We should be able to maintain a holding pattern at double the scheduled time. Over."

"That's a solid copy. Chubby One, out."

Rico Fontana switched the in-flight radio settings to pilot and asked his copilot, "What do you think, Clark?"

Angie Clark responded, "Do you mean, what's actually in those bladders? Well, I'm not sure why a substance developed to cure the UC virus requires hazmat suits."

After a momentary pause, Rico said, "Bingo. You'd think they would have tested it and deemed it safe for humans. Why do I feel we're about to make it worse?"

"Fingers crossed it's just our superstitions and not a fact." She paused, then continued, "God have mercy on us all if it makes it worse. The world ends if it does."

The cockpit fell silent and remained so until their radio blared to life, "Chubby One for Chubby Two, how copy?"

"Chubby Two, good copy."

"Fontana, we have a visual on target. Chubby One is moving into position for our first run."

"Roger that, Chubby Two will assume a holding pattern. We'll recon the area for survivors."

Rite swung his C130 to the northwest and banked hard toward Alameda. He bled off altitude and speed as he lined up his first run. The northwest edge of the island filled his cockpit window when something caught his attention.

The DPRK fleet was now located directly in his flight-path. He glanced at his copilot. "Looks like the brown-water navy is invading the island. Be ready on our countermeasures."

Silvia Brent familiarized herself with the activation system. This bird was equipped with a manual countermeasures system, not the automatic system she was accustomed to. It also meant it was her responsibility to detect and react to any incoming threats.

Rite's voice broke over the inflight coms, "Ortiz, arm the sprayers and activate on my mark."

"Roger that, system armed."

At one thousand yards from the island, Rite gave the order to open the sprayers. Ortiz pressed the large green button that could save the world. He crossed himself and recited a quick prayer. Ortiz had his doubts about their cargo; more importantly, about its effect on the infected. He had lost his entire family to the virus. The thought of having them recover, to be able to hold them in his arms again filled him with hope. But the government's cloak-and-dagger approach had dampened his expectations.

He spoke to no one, "Please, God, let them get it right this time."

CHAPTER 7 – WEAPON

The fleet had embarked on a mission to locate and secure fuel abandoned at any of the marinas and shipyards located around the island city. They moved to a position eight hundred yards northwest of the mouth to Oakland Estuary. A recon team had been assembled and was boarding an air-cushioned landing craft when the alarm sounded.

Packet ordered Choke to determine the cause of the ear-splitting alarm and report back to him immediately. He would remain with their *guest* to ensure her well-being.

Choke burst from the cabin and rushed towards the bridge as the klaxon blared through the crowded decks of the *Bu Gang*. Sailors and soldiers scattered in every direction, some seeking safety, others hungry for orders, all of them slowing his progress.

When he entered the bridge, he followed his crew's gaze. Stunned, Choke watched as the massive airplane descended from the clouds and set a course that would bring them directly overhead. But why would they use the lumbering, unarmed behemoths for their attack? He'd known this battle would come eventually, but military tactics called for nimble warplanes, not cargo carriers.

Ri joined Choke on the bridge shortly after his arrival. He, too, watched the approach of the sun-blocking monster. He glanced at Choke and said, "This is a foolish strategy for the Americans to employ. If it is indeed an attack."

As he finished his statement, a haze formed behind the C130's starboard wing. Choke watched as it coated the main deck's inhabitants in a blue liquid. Panic-stricken at the thought of being poisoned, Choke moved to slam the bridge's door, but he was too late. A fine mist had already entered the tight confines, saturating its occupants.

Choke braced for his body's reaction to the chemical. He turned to find Ri wiping the substance from his eyes. His fearful expression told Choke the general shared his dark thoughts.

Ri ripped the ship-wide broadcast microphone from its cradle and barked a string of commands to the fleet. He ordered them to launch their four remaining helicopters and ready their small cache of IR missiles for launch against the enemy. His time had arrived; his war with the West had begun!

Ri realized the *Bu Gang* was moving on a collision course with the island city. He turned to face the ship's captain and found a frantic man attempting to avoid having his ship destroyed by the enemy aircraft.

"What are you doing, you idiot?" Ri screamed.

The look of horror on the captain's face was the only response Ri received.

"You're going to run us aground..." His words were cut short by the sound of grinding metal. The ship shuttered and groaned in protest as its powerful engines propelled it onto dry land. The *Bu-Gang* pitched hard to starboard. Ri grabbed hold of Choke's suit coat, trying to stop himself from crashing to the bridge's metal floor. He succeeded only in pulling both men to the unforgiving deck.

Bodies twisted into human knots as they slammed against the walls of the bridge while the vessel fought a losing battle against an unyielding opponent.

When the chaos ceased, Choke struggled to his feet. A large gash at his hairline poured blood into his eyes, blurring his vision. Using his hands as his guide, he felt his way to the helm and pulled the EOT (electronic order telegraph) to full-stop.

Choke wiped the sight-stealing liquid from his eyes and blinked rapidly, forcing them to focus. Ri's twisted body was crumpled against the bridge's starboard wall, his neck bent at an impossible angle, leaving no doubt that the man was dead.

Choke's trance broke as the sound of battle reached the bridge. He spun to face the deck. Through the observation window, streaked with blue liquid, he witnessed two men rampaging across the deck, killing anyone in their path. Their movements were those of sleek, deadly predators. The realization pummeled his mind. The weapon he'd created had been set loose upon the *Bu Gang*.

Choke fled the bridge, his body moving on instinct. He pushed past soldiers rushing toward the enemy currently savaging their comrades. Descending the short ladder leading to the captain's quarters, he screamed when a hand gripped his shoulder, spinning him violently towards the unseen attacker.

Choke covered his face, protecting it from the assault to follow, but was shaken violently instead. Packet's voice soon followed. "What happened. Were we fired upon? Has RAM's military launched an attack?"

Lowering his hands, Choke responded, "We have run aground. Ri is gone, killed. RAM has infected the *Bu Gang* with the weapon. Get back to the cabin... NOW!"

Packet stood in stunned silence, the information overwhelming him. His mouth opened, ready to berate Choke when a scream from behind locked it shut. He whirled around as the broken body of a DPRK soldier slid to a stop at his feet.

"RUN!" Choke bellowed, pushing Packet towards the safety of the cabin while using him as a human shield against the manmade weapon lurking just out of sight.

Wharton sprang to her feet, retreating to the back of the room, her fear of the men palpable in its tight confines. She held a satellite phone in her hand, a partially dialed number glowing on its display.

Packet and Choke frantically barricaded the cabin door while screaming at one another in their native tongue. Wharton's inability to understand them, coupled with their desperate actions, pushed her over the proverbial edge.

"Speak English, both of you, speak English!" She paused, her wild-eyed glare bouncing between her captors. When they didn't respond, she screamed, "I said, SPEAK ENGLISH!"

Her shrill tone caused Packet to spin in her direction, fear dominating his features. He charged the woman cowering in the room's shadows, stopping inches from Wharton's face. His broken English filled the room. "We have been overrun. Make the call."

Her confused look enraged him. "The phone in your hand; you were calling for help. Were you not?" Packet grabbed her hand and forced it to her face, slamming the phone against her nose. "Make the call, or I'll feed you to the monsters roaming the halls."

Stunned by the blow and overwhelmed by thoughts of dying at the hands of the monsters outside, Wharton began to cry.

Her reaction sent Packet into a frenzy. He grabbed the sobbing woman and shoved her into the barricade. "Make the CALL!"

His action removed all doubt; he would feed her to the monsters if she disobeyed. Wharton brought her trembling fingers to the phone's keypad and finished dialing.

CHAPTER 8 – CHUBBY TWO

Chubby Two settled into a holding pattern as Chubby One made its second pass on Alameda. Positioning Chubby Two to the west of the DPRK fleet afforded Captain Fontana an unobstructed view and would allow ample time to react to any threats launched by the brown-water navy below. Air Command had pressed forward with the mission after Chubby One encountered no hostilities during its initial run over Alameda.

With the potential threat located off his port-side, he made a snap decision. "Angie, take the controls. I'm going to scan for threats." He quickly located the countermeasures controls and readied himself to deploy them the instant he detected a threat.

Angie Clark moved on instinct and quickly assumed control of the C130. "I have control, Captain. Continuing our current heading."

Fontana didn't acknowledge his first officer's confirmation, his eyes locked on the activity below. It appeared the DPRK fleet was on high alert. But something seemed wrong. They were scurrying about the ship's deck, more panicked than he'd expect in the absence of an actual attack.

It stunned him when the freighter suddenly thrust forward and ran aground. The violent action severed the enormous towlines connected to the remainder of the meager fleet. Fontana moved his hand to the countermeasures control when two helicopters lifted from the Nampo-class frigate. He watched in amazement as the Mil Mi-24s hovered several hundred feet above the deck, then whirled out of control.

The first to take flight suddenly plummeted towards the undersized frigate and crashed through its deck. Moments later, an enormous explosion ripped through the ship, engulfing it in flames.

The second Mil Mi-24 struggled to right itself, then veered hard to starboard, on a collision course with the large freighter. It pitched nearly vertical alongside the ship, abruptly pivoted, then rammed the ship's forward hull. The heavily armored copter ripped through the thick steel, leaving it jutting from the ragged wound.

Something was wrong. As fanatical as they were, the DPRK troops were a disciplined force that would not descend into chaos at the sight of two unarmed heavy transport planes.

"Clark, on our return pass, bring us in closer to the fleet."

Incredulous, Clark responded, "Captain? Are you sure about that?"

Fontana bristled but understood why Clark would question his order. He glanced at his copilot and said, "Bring us in close. Something's happening on those ships…"

An enormous explosion erupted from the freighter, silencing Fontana. The C130 shuddered as the shockwave overtook Chubby Two. Fontana turned back to the window in time to witness a towering fireball mushroom from a jagged breach in the ship's deck.

Broken bodies littered the burning deathtrap. Fontana watched in horror as the remainder of the freighter's crew jumped from the ship's aft. They plunged into the frigid waters of the bay, quickly disappearing into its murky depths.

"Holy shit!" Fontana exclaimed.

An unfamiliar voice quickly filled the speakers in his headset. "Chubby Two, this is Air Command. Abort. Drone surveillance has determined that the target is no longer safe for low-level operations."

"No kidding. Air Command, what's happening down there?"

It surprised Fontana when Rite's voice broke over the radio, "Fontana, the world just ended."

CHAPTER 9 – BE WELL

The relentless pounding on the cabin door made it impossible for Wharton to hear. Edging closer to a complete mental collapse, she screamed, "President Train, I can't hear you. Speak up."

A static-garbled reply eked from the phone's small speaker, "Madam President. You seem to be experiencing some distress, a lot of distress, actually, a great deal of distress. What do you expect me to do about it?"

The door buckled, forcing Packet and Choke to cower against the cabin's far wall, strategically positioning Wharton as a human shield.

"Train, listen to me. Stop playing your juvenile games. As a Head of State, I'm demanding you send an extraction team for me."

Sounds of screaming metal and a violent shudder that nearly threw her to the floor interrupted Wharton's plea. "Oh God, Train. I need your help. Please send a rescue team. PLEEEASE!"

She screamed when Packet's icy fingers laced into her hair, yanking her head to his mouth. "Get us out of here or you'll be the first to die." He shoved her forward as her sanity broke.

She tried to speak, to scream at Train, but only managed to sob uncontrollably into the phone.

Hope soared through her when Train spoke. "Wharton, control yourself. I'll call Mallet to arrange your extraction. Hold for instructions."

"Oh God, thank you, Train."

She glanced at the door, her blurred vision registering the large crack forming in the frame. Wharton stepped back, then again and again until she felt Choke's hands grip her waist. He shoved her forward, slamming her into the haphazardly constructed barricade.

"Train, where are you?" she screamed into the silent phone.

"I'm on the line, Madam President. It seems our troops are busy at the moment. Mallet said something about fighting a ZOMBIE APOCALYPSE. He suggested you work with your military. Or, and stay with me here, work with your allies from North Korea. I hear they have a fearsome military."

"No, no, please listen to me. I need your help. YOU SON OF A BITCH! I need help."

"Madam President, seems to me you got exactly what you asked for, exactly the thing you wanted. Be well, Wharton."

Wharton's sobs filled the room as the door lost its fight against the monsters in the hall.

CHAPTER 10 – RANDY

"Otto Hammer, answer me!" Randy screamed into his radio, receiving only static as a response. His frustration and anger merged into fear. His best friend, his brother, was missing. Randy yanked on Ma Deuce's charging handle, preparing her to re-enter the fight, only to realize she had run out of ammo.

The revelation pushed his rage to the forefront, allowing it to seize control of his actions. Grabbing his AR, he crawled atop his truck's cab and took up a position next to the silent M2 and opened fire. He screamed through each stroke of the trigger, fighting the urge to plummet headlong into the herd and tear them apart barehanded.

Tears stung Randy's eyes as he thought of his friend. Had he suffered a terrible death at the hands of the monsters attacking his home? His sight went fuzzy as his mind wandered.

November 3rd, 2018
Knots Diner

Two eggs over easy, four strips of bacon, and rye toast with butter and grape jelly. It's the same every Saturday. Why does he order the same damn meal every Saturday?

Randy decided to ask Otto just that question. He leaned close to Stone and whispered the question into his ear.

Unfazed, Stone glanced up from his food and asked, "Otto, Randy wants to know why you order the same food every weekend? He thinks it's a sign of someone who fears change."

Randy gave a stiff nod of approval that Stone had relayed his question accurately.

Otto stopped short of taking his first bite of the delicious combination of breakfast food on his fork. The precise combination had been honed over years of experimentation. He glared at Randy, torn between his food and yelling at his friend. He chose the former and ignored him.

Incensed, Randy again leaned into Stone and whispered another question. Stone, seeming to enjoy the situation, finished chewing and said, "Otto, Randy also wants to know why you eat your food the same way every single time? He thinks you're a weirdo."

Otto let his fork fall to his plate and sat back in frustration. He locked his friend in a hard stare and said, "Randy, for God's sakes, man. This is the first time in years I've managed to outshoot you. Hell, maybe ever." A nasty grin broke on Otto's face before he continued, "I'll try harder to let you shoot better than me. I'd hate to *trigger* you again."

Randy's eyes bulged, threatening to burst from their sockets. Stone exploded into laughter, and Otto displayed his smug *I got you* smirk on his face. Randy's mouth worked like a cow's chewing cud, searching for the words that would deliver a devastating response to his friend's insult.

The dials clicked; he readied to hurl his response when the picture window, facing the street, exploded.

The trio shot to their feet, searching for the cause. Expecting to find a driver that had confused the gas and the brake pedals and plowed into the small diner, what greeted them wasn't an accident. A man with a black pirate-style patch over one eye sat atop Randy's truck, a small pile of bricks next to him.

The damage to the paint job on Randy's truck sent him into a frenzy. He bolted for the exit, passing stunned diners along the way. He reached the door as the man began yelling, "This establishment was reported by one of our protection club members. Our member asked us to remind all of you, and the owners of this fine little restaurant, that the American Flag remains a symbol of hate and oppression. This restaurant refuses to acknowledge that simple truth and continues to display it. Your patronage of Knots Diner means you support the oppression of people far and wide. If they cannot enjoy their lives, you cannot enjoy your meal."

The one-eyed man slid from the hood of Randy's oversized vehicle, brick in hand. He hit the ground, reared back, then launched it at the shocked faces staring at him through the diner's shattered window. Randy was only feet from the man when the brick went airborne, and he jumped to intercept the potentially deadly flying object.

His gigantic frame stretched to its length as he slapped the brick to the ground. Momentum took control; Randy twisted off balance and slammed to the sidewalk with a whoosh as the impact forced the air from his lungs, sending the PC enforcer into uncontrollable laughter.

His mind cloudy from the fall, Randy got to his knees, struggling to catch his breath. He glanced at the one-eyed man, now bent over from laughter, and said, "Get your pirate-looking ass away from my truck."

His statement cut One-Eye's laughter off as he went rigid with anger, then turned to grab another brick. He held it over his head, aiming at Randy's skull. Suddenly, a flash of movement entered Randy's vision a split second before a black-and-red-flannel-covered blur collided with the PC member, sending him to the ground. The hollow thunk of the enforcer's head connecting with the asphalt made Randy flinch. *That's going to leave a mark*, he thought.

A tangle of arms and legs scuffled on the ground in front of his truck. Still hazy, Randy wasn't entirely sure what was happening. His confusion cleared when he heard Otto slinging insults at the one-eyed man. His friend abruptly wrestled into position atop the pirate, pinning his arms to the pavement under his knees.

"Hey, Long John, if you'd like to avoid an old man beating you into submission, stop moving." Otto's threat seemed to register. Long John went still, but he continued to glare up at Otto.

A crowd gathered around the men, but no one moved to separate the combatants. Actually, they began egging Otto on.

Winded, Otto said, "I'm going to stand now. If you move, even twitch your finger, I'll poke your other eye out. Clear?"

The man nodded. But everyone knew what would happen. And it did. The moment his arms were free, he swung at Otto. Expecting the move, Otto easily deflected the feeble attack, shifted his full weight to the man's chest, and pummeled Long John with a bone-crushing right cross.

"Now see, that was a bad idea, friend. I was trying to be nice. To let you salvage the small amount of dignity you had left. But nooo, you still want to fight."

Now on his feet and standing next to Stone, Randy sensed it before Stone verbalized it—Otto was losing control. It wouldn't end well for Long John. As deserving as he was of being beaten unconscious, they couldn't allow Otto to do something he'd regret.

Otto confirmed their fears as they moved through the crowd to retrieve him. He launched into a tirade as he pounded Long John's face. "You people have ruined this country. You've destroyed people's lives, tried to silence us, erase us from history. America is splitting in two because of you and your ilk. And you ruined my favorite flannel!"

Otto raised his right fist high above his head, readying another devastating blow when Stone grabbed it. Otto spun, thinking another PC member was attacking him. The fury left his body when he locked eyes with his brother.

"It's time to go, Otto. That punk won't be bothering anyone for a long time. You made sure of that."

Otto understood the message. He was on his way to getting arrested, or worse, killing a man. It wasn't worth it. He got to his feet, using Long John's chest as leverage. He nodded and followed his brother through the parting crowd to Randy's truck. Some half-hearted cheers followed him.

Randy stood at the passenger door, blocking Otto from entering. He found Otto's eyes and said, "I could have taken that punk."

With a sideways grin, Otto replied, "You could've, but I needed to release some pent-up anger."

Randy nodded and wrapped Otto in a bear hug. He didn't speak, but he had just thanked his friend for saving his life.

A hard tug on Randy's arm broke the moment.

***

"Randy, what's wrong. What are you staring at?" The voice belonged to Nila. Her eyes searched his for an answer.

"We need you back in the fight, Randy."

Shocked back to the present, Randy met Nila's stare and said, "He can't be dead, Nila. He just can't be."

CHAPTER 11 – DULL EDGE

I've been told that a sharp knife slicing through skin doesn't hurt as much as a dull knife. So, Long John's knife must have been a dull-edged butter knife, or maybe a plastic knife he got with his last Happy Meal. Whatever the style, it hurt. It hurt like a son-of-a-bitch. So bad, in fact, that my mind tried to freeze up, tried to lock my body to keep it from sustaining more damage.

I realized I couldn't allow that to happen. I'd die if I did.

The single reason I wasn't already dead was that I had a split-second to react to Long John's attack. I pivoted to the right, my move causing the dagger to go wide of its intended target: my gut. Instead, I endured a no less painful glancing *slice*. The dagger easily penetrated my tee-shirt before lacing open the flesh on my left side, just above my belt, then continued forward and opened a gash on my flailing left forearm.

It was going to take dozens of stitches to seal the wounds, but I was alive and still in the fight. Bleeding like a stuck pig, screaming like a madman, but in the fight.

Long John howled in frustration when I latched onto his arm with my left hand and used his momentum to slam him to the ground, jarring the dagger from his grip as I landed on top of him.

Our bodies tangled together, each of us wrestling for control, struggling to live. Suddenly, my blood-slicked hand slid from his wrist. He seized on the opportunity and wedged his now-free hand between us, flipping me onto my back and climbing on top of me, where he straddled my chest.

But I got lucky. He didn't immobilize my arms; instead, he lurched forward, attempting to grab his dagger, which remained just out of reach.

His move placed his left arm hovering over my right arm. He strained to reach the weapon while simultaneously keeping me pinned to the ground.

"You made this too easy, Long John," I said as I launched my fist at his strain-filled face. Not able to generate enough power to inflict the amount of damage I intended, my blow only stunned him. But it was enough for me to seize control of his arms and lock him in place.

As Long John struggled to free himself, I realized that I was faltering. My strength sapped from exertion and blood loss, I needed to catch my breath, to give my body a minute to regroup.

"Hey, seems we're caught in a Mexican standoff. So, while we wait for one of us to make a move, I need some questions answered."

Long John didn't reply, so I plowed on with my one-sided conversation, "Who is Herbert? And why won't he help you? I mean, I'm assuming he's your friend, but he doesn't seem to care all that much about you."

My questions froze Long John. He locked me in a bulging-eyed glare. His heavily damaged face twisted with rage as I admired my handiwork. I had him where I wanted him and pressed forward, "Do you know you're crazy? I mean, you were literally talking to yourself in two different voices. Creepy, right? Nobody does that. Well, crazy people do. That takes me back to my first question. Do you know that you're crazy?"

Long John remained silent. Time for my next question, "You look as bad as you did the first time I smacked you around. Do you remember?"

No response.

"Well, I'm surprised. I'm not easily forgotten. Let me remind you."

***

Bobby's mind filled with static. The old man's vice-like grip locked his arms in place, preventing him from escaping or attacking. He wanted the man, no, *needed* the man to stop talking. To stop prattling so Bobby could think. But he just wouldn't shut up.

The story he told about the first time they'd crossed paths crushed Bobby. The day this old man had humiliated him, beaten him to within an inch of his life. He'd left Bobby battered and bleeding on the pavement in front of Knots Diner. After a week in the hospital, recovering from the thrashing, he'd faced relentless ridicule from his other Protection Club members.

And it was happening again!

Suddenly, his mind cleared enough for him to speak, the words muddled and weak, "Herbert was my half-brother." The memory of his brother sent shards of jagged glass tumbling through his mind. Bobby's world began collapsing around him. His body shuddered. His breath came heavy through a bloody mouth as shattered ribs screamed at him to quit. But quitting meant failure, and failure meant death. Not prepared to die, Bobby prepared to claim his pound of flesh.

CHAPTER 12 – ENTITLED

Willis stood motionless after the neon-green-nailed woman helped him to his feet. Her words still rang in his ears. *The world is depending on me.* The thought promised to crush him.

He spun, attempting to get his directional bearings. His anger peaked when he found the sign pointing him to the VIP housing. The young woman was right. He shouldn't be at Fort Riley—he should be leading his men, making a difference.

Willis stormed towards the address printed on his orders, intending to make his feelings known to the people responsible for taking him out of the fight.

A man clad in black, insignia-free ACUs stood guard at the door as he approached. In no mood for military formalities, Willis simply held the papers up for inspection.

The guard nodded and seemed to share Willis' frustration with the events that led them to be standing face-to-face when he said, "Her majesty awaits."

Willis returned his nod and pushed through the door to find his *assignment* clad in tight-fitting workout gear shadow boxing to an instructional video. She stopped mid-jab at the intrusion, striking a pose meant to impress those around her.

"Sergeant Willis, it's good to see you again. I'm ready to begin my *real* training,"

"It looks to me like you're already training. Tell me, how many soldiers risked their lives for that ridiculous DVD?" Willis tilted his head towards the video still playing on the large television before continuing, "Do you understand what's happening outside your safe little world?" Willis paused, waiting for an answer. When none came, he continued, "People are dying. People I should be helping fight against the dead instead of catering to an elitist snot."

Unaccustomed to being spoken to in this manner, Debbie, the VP's daughter, went red with anger. Her posture stiffened as she glared at Willis. "What's your problem, Sergeant? I want to train with the best this country has to offer. To learn to fight and lead like a warrior."

Willis cut her off, "And do what? Join the soldiers on the front line?" He searched the woman's eyes, waiting for an answer.

Debbie offered no response, just a hard stare.

"That's what I thought. You want to be the person giving orders. You planned to wear my training like some sort of badge. Use it to gain access to the talking heads running this war from the same equally safe distance as you enjoy today. Just like you've done your entire life. You may have changed your name, proclaimed your disgust with your father's politics, and positioned yourself as a champion of the *oppressed*. But you know damn well that you rode Daddy's coattails your entire life."

Debbie remained silent. She wanted to correct him, to prove his statement wrong and embarrass him. But he was right. She was exactly the person he'd accused her of being. Her visions of sitting at the command table shattered as his words sank deep into her psyche. Her shoulders slumped in resignation, her mouth opening to apologize.

But Willis, chest heaving, his anger balanced on the edge of violence, cut her off. Maintaining his withering stare, he said, "My home is being attacked as we speak. If one of my men, or my family, or friends gets killed, I will hold you personally responsible. Good day, miss."

Willis turned abruptly and exited. The man in black displayed a wide grin, then saluted Willis. He returned the salute and headed towards McMaster's office, determined to make his time away from his home mean something. He felt like he was on fire, his brain sending a million signals to his tightly coiled body.

Willis stormed up the Command Building's walkway and flung open the door. The young lady that had helped him to his feet less than thirty minutes earlier was seated at a desk filling out a Form DD/4. She glanced up and met Willis' questioning stare.

"You keep filling that out and you'll be saluting me soon," he said as he walked past her.

With a determined set to her jaw, she stood and saluted Willis. "I just finished."

Willis stopped, turned to face her, and nailed a perfect salute. He grinned and said, "You need to work on that salute, soldier."

McMaster interrupted them as he exited his office. Taking in the scene, he regarded Willis and asked, "What can I do for you, Sergeant? If you're here about your transfer back to Hopkins, you're a tad early. It's going to take several days to get word back on the request." He then glanced at the former anarchist and, in a booming voice, said, "Why are you still standing here, soldier? Report to the In-Processing building. NOW."

Recovering from the flinch-inducing order, she asked, "Sir, where is the In-Processing building located?"

Willis knew what was coming and tried to stifle his laugh.

A flash later, McMaster stood an inch from her terrified face. "Your first task is to locate the In-Processing building. We are not here to hold your hand, soldier. Our job is to turn you into the perfect killing machine. You have exactly two minutes to report to that building. If you arrive half-a-second late, I will have you cleaning latrines for your entire enlistment."

Her response was swift and exactly as it should have been. She spun on her heels and shot through the door, searching for the building that would signify the start of her new life.

McMaster turned to face Willis, ear-to-ear grin on full display. "Again. What can I do for you, Sergeant?"

Willis' anger flared, but he stuffed it. This situation wasn't McMaster's fault. "Sergeant Major. I've recently had a change in my availability. I'm reporting for duty."

"Your timing is impeccable, Willis. You can join me for a meeting at the TOC."

CHAPTER 13 – LISA

Determined to save the woman he loved, Dillan dragged Lisa over the pavement to an abandoned security vehicle. He intended to take her directly to the clinic himself. Waiting for the pickup truck acting as their ambulance was out of the question.

"Dillan, what the hell are you doing?"

"I'm trying to save your life, Lisa."

"STOP! First: You're giving my ass road-rash. Second: Not a chance I'm done fighting."

Her words stopped Dillan in his tracks. His anger at Lisa's bullheadedness flared. "We don't have time, Lisa. You're bleeding like an open spigot, for God's sake. You've been shot. Do you understand what that means? A bullet went into your body! You're going to the damn clinic."

Unfazed, Lisa countered, "Honestly, if it wasn't for the pain, I wouldn't even know someone shot me."

Sliding a hand down his face, Dillan asked, "Do you hear yourself? Seriously, do you?"

Lisa, not happy with her obvious verbal blunder, ran out of patience. "I'm staying here until we get this under control. Have I BEEN CLEAR!"

Dillan knew he'd lost; Lisa seemed determined to kill herself!

"Okay, Slim. Now that I have your attention. Listen up. Go into my left vest pocket. Find the Quick Clot gauze packet. Place the gauze on the wound. You'll find an emergency roll of duct-tape in that same pocket. Use it to cover the holes."

"Are you kidding me? You want me to duct-tape a bullet wound?"

Eye's full of fury, Lisa said, "No, ya dipshit! I want you to duct-tape the gauze to it. Do you understand that my right hand is uninjured? Don't make me use it on your handsome face."

Dillan stopped talking. Lisa was just growing more agitated every time he opened his mouth. A smile creased his features as he thought, *This is why I love her.*

He got her into a seated position and unzipped her vest. The heavy round had easily penetrated its Kevlar lining. He held his breath as he pulled the vest away from her back. If he didn't find an exit wound, he would have to drag her kicking and screaming to the clinic.

His head dropped in relief when he found the bullet wedged in the Kevlar lining. But Dillan's relief quickly faded when he cut her Tru-Spec combat shirt away from her skin. The area around the entry wound appeared badly swollen and heavily bruised as blood flowed freely down her body. But it was the exit wound that caused Dillan's breath to hitch. The jagged hole was easily twice the size of the entry wound and bled profusely.

He again attempted to object, but Lisa cut him off. "Slim, now's not the time to be checking out my sexy body." Her delivery was softer as fear found its way into her voice. She realized that her choice to stay and fight could be her last.

With more dread than he'd ever seen in her eyes, she said, "Stop perving on my boobs and wrap me up."

With trembling hands, Dillan had her patched up in under two minutes. He had tried to inflict as much pain as possible, hoping she'd pass out. But his attempts only served to steel her determination to rejoin the fight. When the stream of blood slowed to a trickle, he re-secured her vest and pulled her to her feet.

Wobbly and pallid, she took a moment to adjust to being vertical. When Randy's screams rang in her ears, her body stiffened. It was a call to action. Still pasty, but able to stand on her own, Lisa flapped the fingers of her right hand into its palm in a "hand it over" motion.

"What are you asking for?"

"I've got to secure my hand to my gun. Give me the tape."

Incredulous, Dillan fished the miniature roll from his pocket and slapped it into her outstretched hand. He thought about offering to help, but he already knew what response that would elicit. He watched as she struggled with the maneuver, fighting both her pain and the tape until she was finally able to wrap her hand several times.

She glanced up at Dillan, meeting his stare and said, "When I reach the fence, I'll need your help sticking the barrel through the links. Then find a gun and start shooting!"

A moment later, Dillan stood next to the woman he loved, unleashing hell on the dead.

CHAPTER 14 – DARLINE

"Natalia, I need ammo at the North Barrier. It's getting hairy over here."

"Darline, this is Natalia. What caliber?"

"5.56 or 223 Rem. Otto's Ruger can accept both. Bring some 9mm as well."

After a long pause, Natalia responded, "Have you been able to contact him?"

Darline hadn't. She needed to remain focused and on task. Thinking about her bullheaded husband would only cloud her thoughts. She was exhausted and sore from the relentless battering to her shoulder from Otto's AR. Her wrists were cramping, her ears rang like church bells, and she was drenched in sweat. If she allowed images to enter her mind of the last time she'd seen her husband, running headlong into certain death, she'd surely crumble.

She thumbed the talk button. "No. He got himself into this mess. He'll need to get himself out of it. Do you have the ammo?"

An uncomfortable pause greeted her. She prepared to repeat the question when Natalia said, "We do. Give us ten for your resupply."

Darline clipped the radio to her belt. Anger and worry seeped in around the edges of her emotional wall. She glanced back to the battlefield. The sight spurred her to slam the door on her feelings; she had a job to do. Dropping the PMAG-30W magazine from the Ruger, she counted five rounds. Her Steyr had one full, fifteen-round magazine left. She'd be out of ammo long before Natalia arrived with her resupply.

"Well, standing around waiting for the ammo fairy isn't going to help anyone," she said to no one. Her words propelled her to action. She pulled the Ruger tight to her battered shoulder and braced for the painful recoil of the powerful rifle.

She lined up a monster when it suddenly exploded into a bloody mist. Her confusion quickly cleared when the massive dump truck filled the Ruger's scope. Raising the rifle's optics up to the cab, she found Pat and Jackson smiling at her. She grinned in response.

Darline yanked the radio from her belt and pressed the talk button. "Darline for Jackson and Pat."

Pat's voice responded, "Pat here. Hold your fire, Darline. We heard you radio for ammo. Thought we'd offer our help." She paused a tick, then continued in a voice just above a whisper, "You gotta try this. I've never had so much fun."

Darline laughed at Pat's childlike enthusiasm. She lowered her gun to watch the devastating power of the big International dump truck rumbling through their enemy.

Jackson zigzagged through the UC horde, destroying the dead by the hundreds. At this rate, Darline wouldn't need more ammo. Her mind slipped to thoughts of Otto. This was his strategy, and it was brilliant.

Her thought snapped when Randy's voice blared from the tiny speaker, screaming for Otto to answer him. Darline held her breath and waited for Otto's voice to respond, to tell them he was alive and coming home. But all she heard was the chatter of a community frantically defending itself.

She couldn't help herself and pushed the talk button. "Otto, please tell us you're alive."

A single tear streamed down her face when Otto didn't answer.

Suddenly a voice rose above the truck's growling engine, breaking her thoughts. "Darline, let's do this!"

She searched for the voice's owner and found Kit working a pike through the fence. Darline knew what she had to do. She locked away the thoughts of her husband and joined her sister-in-law. The battle wasn't over!

CHAPTER 15 – PEARLY GATES

I heard the fear-strained voices of my friend and wife calling to me. I wanted to reply. But I was preoccupied trying to stop Long John from killing me.

I asked, "What's your name?" Then realized I didn't care. "Never mind. I'll just call you Long John."

Similar to countless other times in my life, my voice appeared to have an extremely negative effect on my one-eyed opponent. His body shuddered as his efforts to free himself from my grasp intensified.

Unfazed, I plowed on, "Tell me about your brother. Specifically, why he abandoned you. That's the part I don't understand. Why's that, you ask? Well, my brothers are searching high-and-low for me, because they care about me. If they find you, they will kill you. But Herbert, that guy left you to die."

My observation fueled a fresh rage in Long John. His breathing came hard and fast, spewing bloody spittle through the air. He pulled hard against my grip as his body thrashed, attempting to wrench free.

I was in trouble; I wouldn't be able to hold him much longer. My body was surrendering to exhaustion as my mind rationalized my death as the inevitable outcome of trying to survive a zombie apocalypse.

Long John's unfocused eye signaled it was time to act. I glanced over his shoulder, fixed my stare on a picture hanging on the wall, and said, "You must be Herbert?"

One-eye went stiff, then twisted to greet his savior. I mustered my last threads of strength and landed a vicious blow to his throat.

I found the sensation of his windpipe collapsing under the force of my fist morbidly gratifying.

His panicked gasps quickly filled the room as he tumbled to the floor. He clawed at his neck, trying to remove the hands strangling the life from his body. His eye filled with terror when reality found him. My hands weren't there. He was choking to death.

I struggled to a sitting position, but that was all I could muster. My own reality began setting in after I noticed the floor where I had been lying was soaked thick with my blood. If I didn't get help, and soon, my death would soon follow.

My vision dimmed as unconsciousness tugged at my brain. I had to move.

Long John choked out his last breath as I struggled to hands and knees and crawled, fighting for every inch I traveled.

I glanced to the shattered door; it seemed miles away. Not a chance I'd make it. My head dropped as acceptance took root. I smiled at the memories of the life I had lived. "Saint Peter, I hope you're going to cut me some slack." I chuckled when I thought of what he'd say when I arrived at the Pearly Gates.

The thought fresh in my mind, a voice suddenly pierced my haze. "What's your name, son?"

Too weak to lift my head, I answered, "Saint Peter, shouldn't you already know my name? I thought you guys had it together up here."

"You must be Otto."

I raised my head, determined to walk into Heaven holding it high. What I saw confused my already muddled mind. A man leaning on a cane stood back-lit in the doorway.

"This isn't what I expected, not at all. Shouldn't I be healthy again? Seriously, where's the warm light, the angels singing? I want the whole shebang, Peter!"

"Otto, I can't help you with any of that. But if you give me your radio, I'll call for help."

Son-of-a... My radio! Never thought to use it to save myself.

"You're not Saint Peter, are you?"

The man chuckled as he knelt at my side. "Nope, I'm Olaf. The youngster guarding the door is Russ. How about that radio?"

"On my belt," I wheezed as my arms gave out and I slammed to the floor, my world going dark.

CHAPTER 16 – HOUSE CALL

McCune slapped the phone to his desk. "Sequestered, my ass. You intend to execute me!" The doctor's mind raced. He had to escape Flocci's men. But escape to where? The world was full of flesh-eating monsters. The answer struck with lightning force. He rummaged through the paperwork and charts littering his desk, his anxiety building with each passing second until he found it. The radio, his single connection to the community that had started his journey down this path, would now save his life.

He needed to convince one person to allow him to enter. McCune selected the community's channel, raised the radio to his mouth and, with as much calm as he could force into his voice, he pressed the talk button.

"This is Doctor McCune calling for Pat. Come in, please."

Nothing.

"Again, this is Doctor McCune. I must speak with Pat."

His radio suddenly filled with the frantic voices of people fighting for their lives. McCune's heart pounded as he listened to the pandemonium coming in bits and pieces through the speaker.

Panic-stricken, he screamed over the bedlam, "I MUST SPEAK TO PAT."

A static-distorted voice answered, "McCune, switch to channel nine."

Hands shaking uncontrollably, the doctor struggled to find the requested channel. He finally located the frequency and spoke immediately, "Pat, are you on the line?"

"Go for Pat. Make it quick, Doctor. I'm a tad busy at the moment."

"Understood. It's urgent that I draw several additional samples of Andy's blood. I must conduct additional tests. We're on the verge of a breakthrough."

Pat spoke forcefully to be heard over the roar of the International 4300's massive engine. "Doctor, you said 'I' must draw the blood. Why you? You've requested dozens of samples from Andy. You sent the military or your staff to collect the sample each of those times."

The question caught McCune off guard. He hadn't anticipated being grilled by the matriarch. Although he should have; Pat had treated them with suspicion since day one.

Grasping for an answer that wouldn't expose his true intention, McCune attempted to deflect. "Pat, I also intend to bring medical supplies, antibiotics, and increasingly rare antiviral medications. With winter on the horizon, so too is flu season."

The maneuver didn't escape Pat. But she weighted the offer of the medications against the risk. It was worth it, but not without some rules. "You can see him. But our people will be present to monitor you and whoever you bring with you. As I've already told you, we will not turn Andy over to your group. Understand?"

"Yes, yes, I understand."

"Oh, one more thing. Bring a surgeon with you. We think we have a potential case of appendicitis we need to address."

"Pat, I'm a board-certified surgeon. I'll be able to tend to your patient."

"Excellent. Andy is currently on a mission with FST1. I'll advise you when he returns and we aren't busy attending to the security of our community."

McCune's knees threatened to drop him to the floor. He had to leave the hospital now; Flocci's men would arrive within the hour. "Pat, due to circumstances beyond my control, I'll be leaving the hospital inside of fifteen minutes. I'll attend to your appendicitis patient while I await Andy's return."

Pat stared at the radio. McCune was afraid of something or someone. His insistence was unsettling. Something was happening, something bad. But again she weighed the benefit against the risk. Prepared to decline his request, she allowed the images of the community's wounded to override her apprehension.

"Very well. But Doctor, travel with an armed escort. A well-armed escort. Arrive at the main gate. The east gate is currently inaccessible. Pat out."

McCune felt a momentary sense of relief; he had secured safe refuge. Now he needed to get there alive. He immediately radioed Sergeant Timmons. This time his deception was more polished.

"Sergeant Timmons, I must secure transport to one of the civilian communities. They have a medical emergency which they cannot remedy without my intervention."

Timmons' agitated voice pierced though the speaker, "Well, Doc. I'm dealing with an emergency too. That thing you created is still alive. I'm not sending my men into that room with that savage."

"Sergeant, I fail to see how that's an emergency. If it's contained, it poses no threat. Correct?"

Sergeant Timmons' booming reply threatened to destroy the tiny speaker in McCune's radio. "Doctor, it has been attacking the observation window since you scurried away. If it weren't reinforced glass, your nightmare would already be roaming the halls of this hospital. But it won't be long until the window fails. This thing has already created several cracks; it's only a matter of time."

McCune's response displayed more confidence than he felt., "Shoot it through the window, Sergeant. Problem solved."

"My soldiers will not shoot through the window. I'm not taking the chance of a single shard of that blood-covered glass cutting my men. But thank you for telling me how to do my job."

Desperate to retake control of the conversation, McCune resorted to surrendering to the sergeant's authority and sense of duty to protect the citizens of his country. "I apologize, Sergeant.

I should have known better. Mine was a foolish suggestion. However, we have living human beings that need my help. Can you secure the area until we devise an adequate plan to dispose of the infected?"

Timmons' gruff response sparked hope in McCune. "We're working on that now. Where do you need to go?"

"Thank you, Sergeant. I'm securing some medication and surgical supplies now. I'll be ready to go in a few minutes. We'll be visiting the community established by Otto Hammer, where Sergeant Willis' family lives."

He hoped the mention of a fellow soldier's family would prompt the crusty war-fighter to action. It did.

"I'll take you. Meet me by the main entrance in sixty seconds."

"Thank you, Sergeant. You're saving lives. Also, I've been told you should be well-armed."

"Always, Doctor. You have fifty seconds left. Move!"

CHAPTER 17 – BIG BOX

Stone took a knee and was blasting round after round into the UCs blocking their path. His attempts to clear a path proved woefully insufficient. They needed more guns concentrating on the area. *What the hell is the team doing?*

As the thought crossed his mind, gunfire erupted behind him. He glanced over his shoulder, and his eyes went wide. The team had formed a circular defensive perimeter, battling monsters approaching from all sides. *Well, that answers my question. We're surrounded.*

Scrambling to his feet, Stone yelled, "We need to move, I'm on point."

The members of FST1 immediately fell in behind their point man. Stone noticed the garden center doors sat ajar. A regular customer at the big box hardware store, he knew that the area held its own exit. He made the call. "Garden Center, now!"

The command spurred them forward. *Time for some offense!*

Tesha moved into position off Stone's right shoulder, adding her gun to the frontal assault. Andy and Will covered their right and left flanks. Their pace left the monsters to their rear at a safe distance, but only if they kept moving. It was a risk they had to take.

As they reached the paint counter, a few hundred feet from their goal, things suddenly bounced sideways.

Stone shouted, "Reloading."

At the same instant, Tesha announced a stovepipe-jam.

"Tap—rack—bang!" Stone yelled while searching his vest.

"No kidding, Stone. The next round is mangled," Tesha countered while slapping the forward-assist, attempting to fully chamber the deformed round. Her action proved futile.

She pressed the mag-release, allowing the troubled magazine to fall to the floor. Tesha pulled the charging handle but couldn't eject the now wedged-in-place bullet. She snapped her spring-assisted Kershaw Leek open, pried the 5.56 round free by its case-rim, slapped a fresh magazine into the mag-well, released the bolt, and rejoined the fight.

The maneuver took under a minute. But it wasn't quick enough. Dozens more UC now flooded their path, stopping their forward progress cold.

Stone scanned the immediate area. They'd been hemmed in.

"Paint counter," Will barked as he bolted past Stone and Tesha.

The rectangular-shaped wide-topped counter would provide separation from the horde. But it would also trap them.

As the team charged for the temporary safety of the paint counter, Andy's anxiety built at the prospect of dying in the cavernous store. He planned on living.

As the members of FST1 tumbled over the counter and took up defensive positions, Andy slammed to a stop in the aisle. "Will, I'll clear a path to the garden center, recon the area, and report back. Cover me."

CHAPTER 18 – MINDFUL OF MA

Albright paced behind the Unmanned Aircraft Systems Operator as she held the UAV in a circling pattern over the community. The images broadcast to Camp Hopkins' TOC were sobering. They showed a community fighting for its life.

Albright had already dispatched a fire team to assist. The team was comprised of two Turreted Humvees, a Bradley Fighting Vehicle, and eleven soldiers. A Black Hawk was refueling and would soon join the fight.

The fire team was being led by Sergeant Lucas. Stevenson and Lewis accompanied her in the lead Humvee, with Anderson manning the turret gun.

Lucas raced along the ravaged streets of the city en route to the community, her driving bordering on recklessness. Her intensity put the soldiers on edge, but they respected her urgency. This community, and its people, meant a great deal to the soldiers. It represented the never-say-die American Spirit. They fought fearlessly and sacrificed much to save their home. They put their shoulders into every challenge they faced and pushed back with a collective force rarely witnessed by these battle-hardened war-fighters. It was the reason Willis moved his family there, and why Lewis and Stevenson intended to do the same.

The cab of the Humvee was silent except for the radio broadcasting the frenetic voices of a community under siege. The voices were familiar, but one rose above the chaos. Dillan choreographed the battle like a veteran strategist, one the soldiers would have followed unquestioningly. His voice was firm and direct while projecting a calm confidence.

"That Dillan's a natural leader. Tell me about him," Lucas said after listening for several minutes.

Lewis' jaw hinged open to fill Lucas in on the young man, when a strained voice pierced the radio.

"FST1 for Dillan. We're being overrun. We need backup immediately."

"Dillan for FST1. Negative on backup. We're under attack."

The men regarded Lucas as the conversation between FST1 and Dillan sounded in the background.

"Stevenson, advise FST1 we are sending backup. Get their location and tell them to fight like animals until it arrives. Let Dillan know RAM's military has joined this fight."

Stevenson radioed FST1 the instant Lucas gave the command. While he relayed the message, Lucas used her shoulder-mounted radio to split the trailing Humvee off then gave them the location when Stevenson relayed it to her.

Her decisive reaction eased the doubt that had been nibbling at Stevenson and Lewis. Till now, they hadn't known what to expect from their new leader. Lucas had just proved they could trust her.

Lucas watched from the side-view mirror as the trailing Humvee broke formation and sped toward its new assignment. Her knuckles went white on the steering wheel as they rapidly closed the distance to the community.

"One mile," Lewis announced.

"Weapons hot, check your kits," Lucas commanded. She nodded when she heard the sounds of soldiers readying themselves for battle.

Talking into her shoulder-mounted radio, Lucas hailed the Bradley's crew chief, "Zahra, move to the west of the community. Engage enemy combatants, living or dead. Follow the perimeter and take up a position northeast of the herd. Be mindful of Ma's line of fire. Only use your M240; keep the Bushmaster offline, unless absolutely necessary. Lucas, out."

The BFV confirmed by breaking hard to the west following the prescribed course.

Lucas navigated the last turn of their route to the community, and the sight stole her breath. Countless UCs massed at the community's gate. Hundreds more lay dead in the streets as their brethren trampled their shattered bodies.

She spotted a massive black truck twenty yards from their position, straddling both lanes of the two-lane street. It would be a perfect location for their boots to set up a firing line. With the amount of gunfire coming from inside the community, a mere hundred yards away, she needed to protect her men from being killed by friendly fire.

Pulling next to the Ram pickup, she ordered Lewis and Stevenson to dismount. When Lewis looked a question at her, she said, "I'm moving closer. I want to get Ma-Deuce within her maximum effective range. You and Stevenson thin the edges of the herd from here, out of friendly fire range. These aren't trained soldiers; I don't trust their fire-discipline. I don't need you becoming a target. Hold your fire until Ma comes online."

Lewis' questioning stare lingered. But Lucas' orders were explicit. He exited the Humvee, followed by Stevenson. The soldiers took up positions to the fore and aft of the truck, ensuring they covered their flanks. Thirty seconds later, .50 caliber rounds were ripping through putrid bodies.

As Lewis brought his M4 to his shoulder, he caught movement to the left of the Humvee. Prepared to provide covering fire for his sergeant, it stunned him to find Lucas had exited the massive war machine, adding her M4 to the fight while using the open door as a shield. He was growing to respect her more and more; she'd never be Willis, but she was proving a worthy replacement.

A flash later, Lewis and Stevenson joined the fight.

Stevenson was positioned at the front of the truck, with his bipod-equipped M4 on its hood. Movement from inside the cab drew his attention and his M4 to the windshield. Expecting to find a ravenous monster and cursing himself for not searching the pickup's interior, instead, he found frightened eyes staring at him from between the bucket seats.

"Hands where I can see them. NOW!" Stevenson barked.

"Don't shoot. I'm not infected."

Stevenson swiveled back to the battlefield and ended a UC straying too close to his position. He pivoted back to the truck's cab and found a teenage boy, hands held high above his head. He was shielding himself behind the front seats, and his expression showed he was in great pain.

"Exit the truck, keep your hands in the air, and lay on the ground. I have neither the time nor patience for bullshit. Move your ass, son."

"Sir, we were coming here to see their medics because of my leg. I can't move, but I promise you I'm not a threat."

The teen's sweaty, pallid face lent credence to his claim of injury. But Stevenson didn't trust him. In this new world, he trusted no one.

M4 trained on the teenager's forehead as he moved towards the door opposite the boy's position in the crew cab, Stevenson said, "Don't move. Not even your eyes." While he sidestepped his way to the door, he yelled, "Lewis, we have a live one in the truck. Cover me until he's secured."

Lewis turned to face his teammate, his features displaying the same shock Stevenson felt with finding the truck occupied. He moved to a covering position and dropped his red dot onto the young man's forehead.

Stevenson pulled the door open, stepped back, and leveled his battle rifle at the boy's chest. Scanning the inside of the crew cab, he found a single Glock 17 resting on the floorboard, far from the boy's reach. Stevenson's eyes continued to track through the interior until they landed on an ankle suffering from a compound fracture as bad as any he'd seen on a battlefield. Tension left his body as the realization that the boy may be telling the truth set in.

The teen shifted, trying to add distance between him and the Glock, but his foot didn't follow. Stevenson winced at the sight and met the young man's eyes. "Why are you here alone? How many traveled with you? Where are they?"

Trembling with fear, the young man said, "They heard the radio chatter about Otto. They went to help him. They left me here in case they ran into a herd they couldn't break through." He swallowed hard and continued, "Please don't kill me."

Sensing the situation was under control, Lewis retook his position and unleashed hell on the dead. The M4's blast caused the boy to flinch, then scream in pain.

Stevenson realized the boy was being truthful. If it were a trap, he'd already be dead. He dropped the M4 to low-ready and, dipping his head at the pistol, asked, "Can you use that?"

The boy nodded, being careful to only move his head.

Stevenson bent forward, grabbed the Glock, and shoved it into the teenager's hand. "Good, you are now covering our six. You see anything creeping up on us, shoot it."

With a heavy sigh, the boy began scanning the landscape behind them as Stevenson retook his position and brought his M4 online.

CHAPTER 19 – STEEL GATE

Andy was running before Will could object. He was on a collision course with dozens of monsters converging on their position.

"Covering fire!" he screamed while shouldering his AR and carefully picking off UCs blocking Andy's path. He was soon joined by the rest of FST1. They launched an unrelenting stream of copper-jacketed death into the herd while Andy bobbed, weaved, and plowed his way through them.

Andy's agility and raw strength astonished Will. He moved like a man who had trained for battle his entire life. When the monsters blocked his way, his gloved fists pummeled them as his shoulders lowered the boom on their putrid flesh. He had become a human sledgehammer.

Andy quickly disappeared behind a wall of rotting flesh, allowing the team to shift their fire to the monsters surrounding them.

"I hope he knows what he's doing," yelled Stone.

Barely audible over the onslaught, Will answered, "Whatever he's doing, it'd better be quick. I'm low on ammo."

Will's gut clenched when the rest of the team echoed his statement. They were running out of time! Will grabbed his radio and hailed Dillan. They needed backup, NOW!

When Dillan answered his request for support, Will wished he hadn't. Their home was under attack.

A voice soon followed Dillan's, and it filled him with hope. "FST1, hold the line! Help is on the way."

At that exact moment, Will realized something. The UCs weren't moving; they seemed confused, as if pondering whether to pursue the easy meal or continue their march for the larger amount of food just out of reach. It defied logic. And it scared the shit out of him!

His thought snapped off as Andy's voice burst from his radio. "Will, the gates have a big-ass padlock on them. The steel is too thick to cut. It looks like someone tried to torch through the padlock with a BurnzOmatic. They didn't get far, and it didn't end well. But it gave me an idea. When I tell you to duck, hit the floor as hard as you can, and cover your ears. Andy, out."

Will asked Andy to clarify, but received static as a reply. *Andy, don't get yourself killed.*

Half a minute later, Andy ran into view carrying a two-pound propane cylinder with a torch head still attached. His intent was clear and prompted Will to act. "Everyone down!"

Three bodies hit the floor in unison as Andy began screaming at the UCs, attempting to draw their attention. The mob turned as one and began shambling in his direction. As they massed around him and closed the gap, Andy tossed the cylinder into their ranks.

He retreated thirty yards and took cover behind a heap of lawnmowers and tumbled metal shelving. On one knee, he leaned around the mess and found the cylinder in his Bravo Company AR's scope.

The monsters kicked the cylinder around like a soccer ball but mercifully kept it in the middle of the throng. All Andy had to do was shoot the tiny green target.

His first trigger stroke shattered the calf of a monster wearing a bright orange vest, sending it to the polished concrete floor and trapping his target under its chin. Seizing the opportunity, Andy adjusted his aim and sent a 5.56 green-tipped round into the thin metal wall of the container. The resulting explosion propelled shards of metal through the monsters' ranks, forcing Andy to pull into a tight ball behind his makeshift bunker.

As the dust settled, the sound of full-auto gunfire pierced the air.

CHAPTER 20 – I KNOW

Jackson glanced at Pat. She sat pitched forward. Her left hand gripped the dashboard, and her right hand white-knuckled the door handle. A wicked grin creased her features, widening every time the mammoth truck claimed another victim. Jackson thought Pat was enjoying herself a bit too much.

He agreed that pulverizing zombies from the safety of the International's cab was the best way to fight the undead. And he found great satisfaction in taking the fight to the monsters trying to overrun their home. But it wasn't something he considered enjoyable.

Jackson shook the thought away. He needed to know what she was plotting. "Pat, are you going to share your plan? Why didn't you tell him we're being attacked?"

Pat spoke without pulling her attention from the carnage they were creating. "Well, Jackson, I'm still working on it. But McCune being here to help with our wounded is my priority. We're not equipped to deal with some of the injuries I've seen. If we don't have a surgeon, people will die. Our friends *will* die."

Jackson couldn't argue. They needed a surgeon. Sabrina and Durrell were only capable of *battlefield*-level medical treatment. Attending to internal damage was beyond their skill set.

"I agree, Pat. But you heard the panic in the man's voice, right? He's afraid of something and he's using our community to escape it. What if he brings whatever he's running from to our front door?"

Pat was silent for a long minute. When she spoke, she avoided the question and said, "We need to make sure the main gate is clear for his arrival. I'll split off from you at that point. We need him, but I still don't trust him. So I'll be on his heels until he leaves. We've cleared enough of the dead from this section. The pike team can handle it from here. Head to the main gate."

Jackson didn't press the issue. He knew she wouldn't answer him. Instead, he turned the battlewagon, carefully avoiding the punji sticks, and prepared for their last pass through the monsters shambling at the north wall.

He stared through the windshield and realized Otto's strategy had worked. Dozens of broken bodies lay before them, no longer a threat to their safety. They had thinned the herd on this side of the community dramatically. Pat was right; it was time to move to the main gate.

Jackson depressed the clutch pedal when movement drew his attention to the barrier. He watched as Darline dismounted from the wall and joined Kit and the others on the pike line.

As he watched the dead fall to their attack, a voice pierced the air. He scanned the area and found Natalia standing in front of her resupply vehicle with her arms raised in a "V" staring at him. Her eyes filled with pride. The sight reminded him that failure was not an option.

He smiled at his beautiful wife, nodded, and slammed the shifter into first gear. The International's diesel roared, lurching the behemoth forward, and promptly stalled. Red-faced, Jackson quickly fumbled with the keys, trying to minimize the damage to his pride. It was too late. He could feel Pat's glare.

"Do any of the Hammer boys have their shit together? If needed, I can teach you the proper way to operate a stick shift. Would that help?"

Eyes closed in frustration, Jackson cranked the truck back to life. "No, Pat. I'm good, but thanks for the offer."

Her smile still wide, she asked, "Tell me something, Jackson. You and Stone turned out pretty normal. What happened to Otto?"

Jackson's laugh held both relief at no longer being the focus of Pat's ridicule and amusement at being asked this question for the umpteenth time over the course of his life.

"Whatever do you mean, Pat? Are you referring to his bullheadedness or his knack for saying the wrong thing at exactly the wrong time? Or is it possibly his resemblance to a loose cannon careening around a wooden battleship?"

With a broad smile, Pat said, "I know, I love the crazy bastard too."

CHAPTER 21 – BFV

The noise forced them to abandon the pack. They had heard it before; it held danger. The others moved deeper into hiding, but the familiar noise would find them and end their hunt.

As one, they fled. This unfamiliar hunting ground ran thick with the living. They would feed, soon.

***

Sergeant Zahra sat perched in the open turret of her Bradley Fighting Vehicle. They had encountered few UCs as they rocketed down the side streets just outside the community's perimeter. The monsters that wandered into their path quickly became tread-mash as the twenty-seven-metric-ton war machine crushed them. *Ammo saved*, she thought with a smirk.

Her anticipation grew as the BFV neared the turn that would take them north and into the fray. Zahra lowered her helmet-mounted boom-mic and said, "Approaching target. Weapons hot."

Thirty seconds later, they were facing north and staring into a herd of about a hundred UCs. The M240C spoke soon after, indiscriminately ripping through the ranks of the dead.

As they raced forward, Zahra realized the people of this community had prepared themselves to repel a large-scale attack from either the living or the dead. The bodies of dozens of monsters littered the area thirty feet from the barrier. Their broken husks were strewn amongst boulders or impaled by sharpened sticks jutting from the ground.

Cheers of the living drew her attention to their right flank. She found half a dozen pike-wielding people celebrating their arrival. A smile creased her face, and she gave a thumbs-up to the battle-hardened citizens defending their home.

"We can't fail these people," Zahra said into the boom-mic.

Corporal Smith, the BFV's driver, sounded in her helmet. "Sergeant, we have multiple targets, northwest. They appear to be hiding!"

"Hiding? Clarify."

"They're sheltering behind a cluster of pine trees. One hundred yards, northwest."

Zahra glassed the area through her Steiner HX binoculars. A flash later, the UC cluster came into view. *You sneaky bastards*, she thought as she watched them move deeper into the cover of the large trees.

"Engage the targets."

Zahra watched as the M240C's heavy rounds pummeled the group. Less than twenty seconds later, the only proof of their existence was a cloud of pinkish-black mist hanging in the air.

"Nice shooting," she barked into the boom, then switched the radio's channel from closed to broadcast and hailed Lucas. "Zahra for Lucas. How copy?"

"Go for Lucas."

"Sergeant, we encountered a cluster of UC using cover. Check your flanks. These bastards just upped their game."

The INTEL chilled Lucas. She immediately scanned the area to her Humvee's left and right flanks. "Team, stay frosty on your flanks. Shit just got real."

Zahra directed the tracked beast to the northwest point of the perimeter, intending to clear stragglers as they made their way to the northeast position as ordered by Lucas. Her focus was on the pine trees where the M240C had decimated the group of UCs using them as cover.

Suddenly the BFV slammed to a stop, jolting Zahra forward into the turret's edge. Angry and startled, she barked into her boom-mic, "What the hell is wrong with you, Smith? If you broke my ribs, I'm going to kick your ass, soldier!"

The sound of rubber skidding on pavement drew her attention to the front of the BFV. Her wide eyes watched an enormous dump truck fighting against momentum as blue smoke billowed from its tires. The truck's ass-end fishtailed as the driver battled the steering wheel for control.

Zahra's order to Smith for a full reverse was cut off when the behemoth screeched to a halt inches from her Bradley.

***

Pat glanced at Jackson, her face white and mouth dry from fear. He was still standing on the brake pedal and fixated on the armored beast sitting inches from the International's front bumper.

"I think I shit myself, Jackson."

"Sorry, Pat. I didn't hear you because I think I blacked out. Are we still alive?"

Pat turned back to the windshield and followed the war machine's 25mm Bushmaster chain gun track upwards. Its business end leveled at the glass she was currently staring through.

"Put your hands up, Jackson. Try not to look like a threat."

***

Four hands and two toothy smiles instantly appeared in the truck's cab. The action prompted Zahra to reverse her order to fire on the vehicle. She unclipped her shoulder-mounted radio and held it and three fingers in the air, representing the channel she wanted them to tune into.

The crazed-looking woman moved slowly and brought a radio to her mouth. A quick burst of static preceded a shaky voice. "My name is Pat Schreiber; the young man is Jackson Hammer. We mean you no harm. We are fighting to save our community. You can check with soldiers by the names of Lewis and Stevenson. They'll vouch for us."

Zahra took in the gore-covered truck replete with makeshift armor. Remnants of its victims hung from thick pieces of rebar, and blood dripped to the pavement. Against its stark white frame, the blood splattered down its side appeared to be a macabre paint job meant to resemble flames, the likes of which adorned hot rods of a bygone era.

The sergeant told Pat to hold and quickly switched to the fire team's channel. "Zahra for Lewis, how copy?"

"Go for Lewis."

"I'm holding two at gunpoint. They claim to live in the community. Can you confirm that Pat Schreiber and Jackson Hammer are friendlies? Over."

"Friendly isn't a fitting description for Pat. But yes, both belong to the community. Whatever you do, don't get Pat angry. She's a scary woman! Out."

Switching back to channel three, Zahra hailed Pat. "I'm Sergeant Zahra. We are here to help you with your fight. Also, you can put your hands down, and please stop smiling. You both look like crazy people. It's making me uncomfortable." She smiled and then continued, "Pat, seems that you've made a lasting impression on Lewis."

"Sergeant, it's good to make your acquaintance. I think you'll agree. Men are soft."

Pat's confident tone had returned. Recovering from the shock of nearly being killed, she refocused on their mission. McCune was en route, and this area needed to be clear when he arrived.

"Sergeant, can you clear the area behind us? It's our main gate, and it must remain secure."

"We'll clear what we can as we pass. Your east perimeter is our primary target. Zahra, out."

With that, the BFV reversed and pivoted to the right and sped past them. A moment later, the sound of full-auto gunfire reached Pat's ears.

Smiling, she glanced at Jackson and said, "Let's get to work."

Chapter 22 – Rude

My body shook violently while someone screamed for me to wake up. My first thought was: *Dad's pissed that I slept in again.* But it's Saturday. I sleep in on Saturdays because I drink too much on Fridays. It's a rule.

Without warning, someone flipped me onto my back. My left side screamed in protest at the abrupt movement. *Dad is really mad today.*

Wanting to end this madness, I hollered, "You're rude! I'm trying to get some rest! I think I have the flu!"

The voice that answered wasn't my father's. "Otto, wake your ass up. We need to get moving."

The unfamiliar voice, coupled with its urgent tone, snapped my eyes open. My blurry vision fell on a man leaning an inch from my face.

"You're not my dad!"

"No, I've already told you. I'm Olaf. Russ is the man guarding the door. Get up, NOW."

It was all coming back to me. I was living in the apocalypse, my home was under siege, I had killed a man and been stabbed, and Olaf had a hundred pounds of venison in his truck.

After several painful attempts, I finally stood on wobbly legs and surveyed my surroundings. The realization hit me; I had gone primeval on the man lying dead mere feet away.

Olaf called to Russ for help. At first, I took offense. *I'm not fat.* Then I remembered his cane and swallowed my rebuttal. Russ scurried into position under my right shoulder, easing the burden on my exhausted legs.

As we headed for the door, a thought entered my woozy head. "So Olaf, is this where we sing…"

Anticipating what I'd say next, Olaf talked over me, "Let it go, Otto. Just let it go."

"Ha, I knew it. Frozen *is* your favorite movie!"

Russ sniggered as he struggled under my weight. Having never spoken to the towheaded youngster, I determined it was time for introductions.

"So, is Russ short for Rusty? I used to drink at a bar called the Rusty Nail. Know the place?"

Russ shot me a bemused look. When he faced me, I noticed the wound adorning his cheek, just below his right eye. The purple bruise surrounding welted flesh looked painful and fresh.

"Whoa, what happened to you, Rusty?"

A look I've grown used to over the years crossed his features. Annoyance. "I was hit by a rock… ya know what? It doesn't matter. Just move your stomps so we can get you home."

After a pause, he yelled, "Olaf, radio his people and ask them if they want him back. I'm guessing they don't, but he can't live with us."

"Hey, I'm wounded too! Worse than you, I might add. And, for your information, they do-so want me back. They've been radioing like crazy. Probably have hundreds of people out searching for me."

Rusty appeared to make ready a response, but Olaf was already on the radio, his voice cutting the towhead off. "This is Olaf for Dillan."

A long minute passed before Dillan responded, "Olaf, your timing is terrible. We can't help you; we're being attacked."

"I know. But I'm with Otto. He needs a doctor, pronto. So does my son."

When Olaf released the talk button, the radio's speaker filled with the voices of my community. One voice surged through the clatter.

"If you hurt him, I'll hunt you down and rip your lungs from your chest. Have I made myself clear?"

Olaf stared at the radio, and his shocked expression morphed into a smile. "You must be Darline. Seems Otto didn't tell you about me. I promise you, Otto's safe."

"Is he hurt?" asked Darline, voice choked with emotion.

"Well, he's making fun of our names. So I'm guessing he'll live. But he'll need some stitches."

Dillan seized control of the conversation. "Olaf, RAM's military has joined the fight. If you encounter them, do your best to appear friendly. Tell them you're acting on my direction. Better yet, can you hold your current position?"

Olaf paused, gripped by indecision. When he finally spoke, his intent was clear. "I need to get back to my truck. My boy is hiding in it."

Suddenly, a familiar voice crackled through the radio's speaker. "This is Lewis for Olaf. We have your son covered. If you can't make it back to your truck safely, don't break from cover. Over."

Olaf had made his choice. "If we retrace our path, we'll be fine." He paused, leaned through the destroyed doorway, assessed the area, and continued, "I only see a few stragglers. The commotion at the wall has their attention. We're heading your way now. See you in five."

"Olaf, radio me when you're approaching. We'll adjust our fire. Lewis, out."

I watched Olaf stuff my radio into a pocket of his oilskin duster. He turned to face us, his features hard. He nodded, stepped over the mangled threshold, and bolted into the late summer air.

His pace threatened to leave Rusty and me dangerously exposed. But his focus remained on getting to his son.

"Olaf, slow down. This guy weighs a ton. I can't keep up."

"Hey, Rusty, easy on your commentary about my weight. It's the damn sodium in those nasty MREs. I'm holding water, that's all. It's just water weight."

Rusty shook his head. "It's Russ, call me RUSS! And I'm telling you I don't care if it's water or blubber; you weigh a ton."

"That's it. I'll walk on my own. Let go of me," I said, struggling to break free of his grip. "Wouldn't want to give the weakling towhead a hernia. Besides, I'm feeling better. My second wind kicked in."

Russ conceded faster than expected. Actually, I didn't expect it at all. The next thing I knew, I was stumbling forward on a collision course with an enormous buckthorn, its giant thorns promising to gouge out my eyes. The thought terrified me, so I did the only thing I could: I stitched them shut, fell to my hands and knees, and screamed for help as I slid over mud-slicked turf toward the thorny beast.

When nothing happened, I slowly opened my eyes, bringing into focus the single largest thorn I'd ever seen. Another inch and the invasive shrub would have claimed my left eye as its latest victim.

I stared, transfixed by the deadly foliage, when hysterical laughter came from my left. It was Russ. The little shit was leaving me to die!

"Hey, little help here. I can walk on my own. Standing is something altogether different."

Russ glanced over his shoulder and yelled, "You better figure it out, quick. Company's coming."

His meaning became clear when the raspy call of a hungry UC reached my ears. Still on all fours, I snapped my head back and forth, attempting to locate the monster. I found nothing. Then realization hit me—it was directly behind me.

Panic in control, I began crawling after Olaf and Russ. Pain from my left side and arm went white-hot, hindering my pace. If I didn't get to my feet and run, I'd get eaten alive.

The same instant the thought of the monster's teeth ripping my skin entered my mind, hands pulled me to my feet.

"Ha, couldn't live without the old man, could ya? We'll talk about you leaving me to die later."

Russ rolled his eyes, spun, and bolted towards a now distant Olaf. "I'm not helping you again. RUN."

It surprised me how quickly Russ turned nasty on me. It usually doesn't happen until you get to know me. But he had a point, I should run.

My body had other ideas. After my first few steps, my run morphed into a lope, then devolved into a limping struggle to move forward. My hamstrings warned me that bad things would happen if I pushed them any harder. But with the UC locked onto me like a heat-seeking missile, and an empty gun on my hip, my only option was to push forward.

The shambling beast matched my pace, through backyards and brush-covered lots, for fifty yards, calling to its food in a language known only to its brethren. I decided it was time to fight.

As I trundled along, my eyes scanned the ground for a makeshift weapon but found nothing. I reached for my radio. Again, nothing. As I cursed Olaf for commandeering my lifeline, I suddenly realized I was standing on a cement sidewalk.

The sounds of battle filled the late summer air as I looked up to find my salvation. A massive black pickup truck, providing cover for two soldiers positioned on either end, sat less than twenty-five yards away. I quickly recognized the nearest of the soldiers as Lewis. The other soldier was using the hood as a firing platform, his face obscured by the truck's cab.

From Olaf's description when we talked earlier in the day, I determined the truck belonged to him. But something was wrong. Olaf and Russ were nowhere in sight.

Approaching the truck from its right flank had me facing its tailgate and put me off Lewis' right shoulder. His attention was focused downrange as I shuffled in his direction. I waved my arms and yelled to signal my approach, but he didn't hear me or didn't care. Either way, the UC was closing on me.

My predicament was becoming clear through my foggy mind. If I startled Lewis, he'd shoot me. If I stopped, the UC would eat me. Gripped by indecision, I froze mid-step. I had to fight.

I sucked in a deep breath, flexed my hands, and spun to face the enemy. "Alright, you son-of-a-bitch, get ready to work for your next meal."

The monster responded by increasing his pace. Claw-like hands reached for me as its maw hinged open in anticipation of tasting my flesh. I took in the pathetic beast's mangled form shambling in my direction. Its ability to walk, to move at all, defied logic. Yet still it hungered for human meat. I squared my shoulders and prepared to fight for my life.

Suddenly its head went airborne, tumbling to the ground at my feet. My confusion soon cleared as the monster's body folded to the pavement, and Olaf appeared, holding a sword in a two-handed grip.

He wiped the razor-sharp blade on the monster's tattered clothing and slid it back into its scabbard, which doubled as his cane. Locking eyes with me, he said, "You didn't think I'd leave you to die, did you?"

"Yeah, I kinda did. It's the part where you left me to die that made me think you were actually leaving me to die."

Olaf shook his head, his eyes never leaving mine. "Otto, you need to have faith, brother."

"Olaf, you took off. Rusty, Russ, whatever his name is, dropped me. Then he ran by me, laughing like a crazy person. You'll excuse me if I doubt you."

"Ah, well. I don't speak for Russ. He probably left you to die. But I was clearing a path for you."

Russ popped up from a low hedgerow a few yards away. "I *was* laughing at you. Not about you being eaten, Otto. You should've seen yourself sliding at that thorn bush. It was a sight. Also, don't forget, you said you didn't need my help, so I didn't help."

"It's a buckthorn."

Russ gave me a quizzical look.

"The thing you called a thorn bush, it's called a buckthorn. It could have poked my eye out."

Russ pushed through the hedgerow, eyes fixed on me. His posture told me to get ready to fight. I brought my fists up, boxer-style, and waited.

I flinched when he brought his hands up, forcing a chuckle from the young man. "You're a skittish one, Otto. Olaf radioed the soldiers; they're waving us over. Believe me; if I was going to hit you, you wouldn't see it coming."

I turned and found Lewis motioning to us to join him. Olaf was already running to the truck, and Russ followed suit. Still unsteady, I tried jogging, but my body requested I walk, slowly.

By the time I joined them, Lewis had refocused on the UC horde massed at the east gate. Seeing the attack from this angle stole my breath. Bodies littered the area around my home. Gunfire filled the air as pikes shattered skull after rotting skull. My friends were fighting for their lives.

I took a step towards my home when a thumping sound filled my ears, and the sun was blotted from the sky.

CHAPTER 23 – FRYING PAN TO FIRE

Doctor McCune clutched his medical bag to his chest as Timmons wheeled the Humvee through the desolate streets of a once thriving city. It was the first time he'd ventured from the safety of the hospitals grounds since Operation Nightingale secured Saint Joe's for his research.

"Doctor, loosen your grip on that bag. You'll be useless if your fingers are broken."

McCune twisted to face Sergeant Timmons. The man's words both startled and confused him. Timmons bobbed his head at the bag. "Doc, your knuckles are white. Any more pressure and fingers will start snapping."

McCune shifted his gaze to the bag and realized what Timmons meant. "I suppose you have a point, Sergeant." He allowed the bag to fall to his lap but felt no less terrified. "How much longer until we reach the community? It's a matter of life or death."

Timmons referenced his map, then glanced over his shoulder. The soldier tapped to accompany them was manning the turret gun, safely out of earshot. "What should I tell them when they arrive at Saint Joe's?"

McCune clamped his eyes closed and lowered his head. "What gave me away?" he asked.

"Doc, I've been a soldier a long time. I know panic when I see it. You packed your bags in seconds flat. You have all of your research in those boxes sitting on the backseats. Judging from the amount of glass clinking around your bag, you've packed enough medication to stock a small hospital. But the thing that stands out? Saint Joe's has, what, a dozen doctors you could have sent in your place." Timmons paused, waiting for McCune to answer. When he didn't, Timmons pressed on, "So, what do I tell them when they arrive. I don't know what you're running from, and I don't get paid enough to care. But you're a good man. You've made some mistakes, but you're still a good man."

McCune, head still bowed, said, "Tell them I'm dead, killed while examining that blue savage in the containment room."

Timmons chuckled. "You're a crafty bastard, Doc."

His levity broke when the M2 barked a burst of death at an unseen enemy. McCune's head snapped up as Timmons lowered his boom-mic and asked the soldier for a sit-rep.

After a long silence, Timmons raised his mic and said, "Buckle up. We're three minutes out."

Eyes bulging, McCune asked, "Why was he shooting?"

"Area's getting thick with UCs. Get used to that sound."

McCune's trembling hands kneaded the medical bag's supple leather. Had he made the right choice? Should he have joined Flocci at the CDC? Did he jump willingly from the frying pan into the fire?

"Doc, if your first instinct was to run. Trust it, it'll keep you alive." Timmons yanked the steering wheel hard to the left, then slammed on the brakes. Mangled bodies littered their route, some struggling to stand despite devastating injuries. An enormous dump truck rumbled in the opposite direction, and it became clear that the beast had caused the destruction laid out before them.

A long whistle preceded Timmons' words. "Holy shit. Now I know why they told you to come heavily armed."

McCune fumbled through the pockets of his coat for his radio. Finding it, he pressed the talk button and hailed Pat. "This is Doctor McCune for Pat Schreiber. I have arrived. Our Humvee is approximately one hundred yards from the main gate. How do we enter the community?"

Before Pat responded, Timmons locked onto the doctor's eyes. "*We* don't enter, you do. Tell them to pick you up. I'm not risking getting trapped here. I have a *meeting* to attend back at Saint Joe's."

McCune nodded his understanding and radioed the update to Pat. The truck's brake lights flared in the distance as the behemoth executed a sloppy U-turn, smashing through unkempt flowerbeds while crushing an unaware monster trudging towards the community. It roared in their direction, arriving next to the battlewagon more quickly than McCune thought possible.

McCune faced Timmons, prepared to thank him. But the crusty soldier suddenly pressed a hand to his helmet, lowered his boom-mic, and said, "Go for Timmons." He listened intently, then ended the transmission with a gruff, "Affirmative. Advise them I'll return in ten. They are not to move until I arrive. Tell them the truth: Doctor McCune died in the containment room. Timmons, out."

Casting a telling look at McCune, Timmons thrust his chin at the door. The doctor nodded his understanding, checked the area outside his door for monsters, and exited the Humvee as Pat swung open the dump truck's passenger door.

McCune slipped into the shoulder strap of the messenger-style medical bag, darted to the Humvee's rear passenger door, grabbed hold of the first of two boxes labeled "Antidote Test Data," and heaved it at an unprepared Pat. The second box was soon airborne, followed by McCune as he scrambled up the side steps, into the cab, and over Pat.

The doctor quickly situated himself on the cramped bench-style seat. Smoothing out his hair, McCune faced Pat and said, "It's a pleasure to finally meet you. Please take me to my patient. Time is of the essence."

Pat, feet now resting atop the boxes, asked, "So, Doctor. Why on earth is all of this stuff needed to perform a routine appendectomy and draw a vial of Andy's blood?"

McCune stared unblinking at her as Jackson eased the truck into gear and wheeled towards the main gate.

After a long silence Jackson added, "Doc, Pat asked you a question."

Doctor McCune closed his eyes, leaned his head back, and said, "I've never mastered the art of deception. Please believe me, I mean you no harm."

CHAPTER 24 – MEN IN BLACK

Timmons fishtailed the Humvee to a stop at the hospital's main entrance. Leaving the battlewagon running and the turret gunner in place, he dismounted and charged through the sliding glass doors. The screaming voices and gunplay echoing through the tiled hallways signaled his orders hadn't been obeyed.

Timmons slammed to a stop in the expansive reception area. He strained to identify the direction of the chaos. Corporal Philips had exited the Humvee and quickly joined him. Their heads pivoted between the three hallways branching off the lobby.

Wide-eyed, the corporal said, "It's coming from the containment area."

Timmons acknowledged Philips by rushing toward the slowing gunfire. Thirty seconds later, M4 at high ready, Timmons sliced the corner to the hall leading to the containment room holding the blue savage.

The sight greeting him boiled his blood. A man in black ACUs stood over a downed soldier, smoke trailing from his gun's muzzle. Soldiers scrambled to put distance between their defensive perimeter and the containment room.

Timmons shouldered his M4 as Phillips broke to their left flank, leveling his battle rifle at the chaos in front of them. With no obvious enemy to fire on, Timmons focused on the man who had obviously killed his soldier. "Drop your weapon, NOW."

The man in black ignored his command, spun on his heels, and disappeared into the containment area. The action spurred Timmons forward, with Phillips holding his position.

"What the hell is happening?" he asked a wide-eyed soldier named Alvarez.

"These two idiots from the CDC tried to enter the containment room. Claim to have orders to secure that thing, and McCune." Her eyes shifted to the downed soldier. "That blue... whatever it is, bit Murphy."

Timmons pivoted towards the room the same instant a knife plunged into the savage's skull. Breathless, the duo turned to face the sergeant, quickly realizing he viewed them as a threat.

"Whoa, ease up. We're on the same team."

"Bullshit," spat Timmons. "If we were on the same team, you would have followed my orders and my soldier would still be alive." He glared at them through his Aimpoint, its red dot resting on the bearded man's forehead. "Identify yourselves. If you tell me you're from the CDC, I will shoot you."

The men exchanged an uneasy stare. Timmons was clear; their next move could cost them their lives.

"Names aren't important, Sergeant." A bearded man, and the obvious leader, began. "Orders are. We're here to retrieve McCune and any of his test specimens. As you can see, we failed in securing the test subject."

The second man tugged on his sleeve while stepping forward. "I'm sorry about your soldier. This thing moved like lightning. It blasted through the door the instant we finished removing the barricade. Your man got caught in its path."

Timmons' red dot now rested on the seconds man's throat. "Out, now! Remove yourselves from my facility. Phillips, escort our *teammates* to their vehicle. Shoot them if they resist."

"You heard the man. Move your asses," said Phillips.

"What about the doctor? Our orders are to escort him to the CDC in Atlanta."

Red dot still trained on the second man in black, Timmons answered, "You're probably standing on him, or parts of him. Like you pointed out, that thing moved like lightning. He was dead in the blink of an eye."

The duo's leader made a show of looking around the containment room. "Funny, we only found one head, which clearly doesn't belong to McCune."

Patience gone, Timmons hard-stepped towards the men and slid his finger inside his M4's trigger guard. "I told you to leave my facility. NOW!"

Phillips pulled his battle rifle tight to his shoulder. "You've got a three-count to move. My orders are crystal clear. One... Two..."

"Alright, alright, we're going. At ease, soldier."

"I don't take orders from unidentified government goons. Step lively, gentlemen."

Timmons was enjoying the exchange. Phillips was a tough nut and wouldn't hesitate to follow his orders. As Phillips stepped aside, allowing the men in black to pass, Timmons noticed that all of his soldiers had trained their weapons on the men. No orders needed. They trusted their sergeant and mirrored his actions.

As the threat disappeared around the corner, his team sprang into action. They secured Murphy's body and re-sealed the containment room.

As he watched them work, the weight of his actions hit him. *God, please don't let this backfire on us.*

***

Donny sat quietly in the passenger seat as Leo radioed in a situation report. Cutting a glance at his partner, he stealthily wiped an increasing amount of sweat from his brow. Pain radiated from his right wrist, intensifying as each second ticked by.

Relief spread over Donny as Leo slid the borrowed Humvee into gear when the transmission ended.

"We've been ordered to search a community about ten klicks south. The CDC suits suspect the good doctor's hiding there."

"Leo, do those idiots realize every single person still alive is armed, some with mil-spec weapons?"

"What's going on, Donny? You've never cowered from a fight."

Donny cut him off. "Look, if McCune's hiding, he knows what's coming. Those people will protect him. I brought two magazines. How many did you bring? Answer? Not enough. This should have been an easy retrieval, no shots fired. Not an assault on a well-defended civilian stronghold."

Leo chewed on the insight; they'd get slaughtered if things went sideways. But the suits had worked themselves into a lather over McCune. Disobeying their orders could prove equally fatal.

"No worries, I'll charm our way past the gate." A crooked smile creased his features.

A guttural growl pulled Leo's eyes from the road. They locked onto his longtime friend a moment before a ghost-white hand snapped his neck.

CHAPTER 25 – M134

Heads ducked for cover behind the community's earthen barrier, and guns fell silent as the Black Hawk settled into a hover just north of the battlefield, a mere hundred feet above blood-soaked terra firma. A second later, the telltale sound of an M134 Minigun filled the air, its 175-grain projectiles pummeling the UC ranks.

Rapt by the display of power, I flinched when an all too familiar voice sullied my ears.

"You look like shit, Hammer."

I snapped around, my side punishing me for the quick movement. Instinctively reaching for my side, I was rewarded with jolting pain for my effort. Finally able to assess the damage to my body, I found a ragged hole in my shirt; it was drenched with blood, which had soaked my side down to my ankle.

"He ruined two of my shirts," I blurted.

"What are you talking about, Hammer?" Lucas asked.

"Long John ruined two of my shirts. One was my favorite flannel and now this one."

Face in palm, sitting in her Humvee's driver seat, its door open, Lucas said, "You're a piece of work. The battle, your wound, the giant helicopter, all those things and it's your shirts you're most concerned about. Really?"

"But… they were my favorites."

Suddenly, the M134 fell silent, pulling our attention to the battlefield and ending our bizarre conversation.

The broken bodies of the monsters, which had been attacking my home only moments earlier, littered the area. The Black Hawk began circling the community's perimeter, disappearing behind a line of mature pine trees, its devastating gun coming online in short, controlled bursts as it mopped up the stragglers from the undead army.

As Olaf tended to his son, with Russ at his side, Lucas exited her Humvee, standing shoulder to shoulder with me. She grabbed her radio. "Lucas for Camp Hopkins, how copy?"

"This is Camp Hopkins, good copy."

"Hopkins, we're going to need heavy equipment. Send two frontend loaders and two dump trucks. We have a lot of shit to clean off the streets. Lucas, out."

As she finished speaking, she turned to face me. It was then she got a clear look at my bloody side. Locking me in a hard stare, she said, "Well, you weren't kidding; that son-of-bitch ruined your shirt."

Returning her bloodshot stare, I said, "Can you even see through those eyes? It looks like the veins would cover your retinas. Worse than cataracts, actually."

As I spoke, I swayed like a flag in a lazy breeze. My vision swam, my thoughts went fuzzy. But Lucas' angry mug burned through my haze.

In a preemptive strike, I asked, "Can you take me home? I'm not feeling so good."

Lucas hard-stepped in my direction, causing me to raise my arms to cover my face. Instead of a right-cross, her arms hooked under my shoulders and pulled me to the back door of the Humvee.

After getting me situated, she said, "People seem to like you. I don't know why, but they do. So, I'm going to stuff my first instinct of leaving you here to bleed out. But I promise you, if you utter one word while I'm driving, ONE WORD, I will take your life. Have I been clear, Mister Hammer?"

When I didn't respond, Lucas appeared to have a psychotic break. "I asked you a question. Answer me!"

Through my foggy stare, I said, "You told me not to speak. Actually, you said you'd take my life if I uttered ONE WORD!

Look, Sergeant Lucas, if we're going to have a solid working relationship, you'll need to work on your communication skills. So which is it, I don't speak, or I answer your question?"

Air pumping through flared nostrils, Lucas sputtered through a half dozen words, then gave up. "Lewis, escort this... this... person to the gate. If they choose to take him back, make sure he gets medical attention. Or not, I really don't care."

The door slammed as she finished speaking. A flash later, Lewis sat in the driver's seat and motioned for Olaf to follow us.

I began voicing my opinion of Lucas when Lewis held up his hand, silencing me. He grabbed the radio and hailed Dillan to let him know he was bringing me home.

CHAPTER 26 – FST1

Andy remained behind cover as the full-auto gunfire raged. He knew FST1 wasn't the source of the barrage. He checked his ammo, shouldered his AR, and prepared to fight the unknown enemy. His grip threatened to crush his rifle's pistol grip. An anger burning deep in his body promised to explode, sending him headlong into the fray. If these people intended to cause harm to his team, they would pay the ultimate price. His legs twitched, ready to carry him to the fight at the same instant the gunfire ceased. The voices of his team called to him, frantic and filled with concern, soon joined by the telltale rumble of a diesel engine growing in volume.

The sound of boots crunching broken glass prompted him to stand. Weapon still shouldered, he swept its muzzle left to right, searching for a threat. When it found Will and Stone, Andy's finger slipped into the trigger guard.

The action didn't escape his teammates, and they dove for cover. "Jesus H., Andy. We yelled clear, and we meant it. The area is all-clear."

Andy could see the beads of sweat rolling down Will's face through his red-dot, his vision crystal-clear through the non-magnified device.

He ignored Will and swung his AR toward the unknown vehicle approaching rapidly from the direction where FST1 had entered the big box store. A confused boyish face filled his Aimpoint's lens.

His mind struggled to break free of its hyper-vigilant state. RAM soldiers packed the Humvee, ones that had, only moments ago, added their guns to the fight. He held his defensive posture for a tick longer before lowering his weapon.

Will and Stone approached cautiously, guns at low ready. "You okay, Andy?" asked Stone.

"Yeah, I'm good. Jacked up, but good. I thought we were about to roll into another fight. I'm good now."

Will kept a suspicious eye on Andy. Something told him his friend wasn't *good*. "I've never seen a man fight like you just did. Where'd that come from?"

Andy searched for an answer to his friend's question. His jaw hinged open, but an authoritative voice coming from the Humvee cut him off. "Gentlemen, we need to move out. We'll escort you back to your home."

Will snapped to attention. Their community was under attack. "FST1, rally at our Humvee. Our home is under siege."

***

Under six minutes later, FST1 was following Lewis' Humvee and an unidentified Ram pickup truck through the east gate. They split from the tiny convoy as it raced toward the community's clinic.

Using the Humvee to block the now open gate, FST1 dismounted and took up firing positions behind the massive battlewagon, covering community members as they killed the last of the undead, giving dozens a second death as their bodies flailed on the defensive obstacles laid out before the barrier.

Stone peeled off and searched the faces of the community's defenders. Hollow eyes stared back as he made his way along the barrier. A grim smile broke his hard features. Their defenses had held!

As he walked, anxiety took hold. He wasn't finding the faces that mattered most to him. He stopped cold when familiar voices rose above the murmurs of the warriors surrounding him.

"Lisa, you're going to the damn clinic. NOW!" Dillan yelled.

"Watch your tone, Slim," answered Lisa, voice full of anger.

"Don't make me use this tone, Lisa, and you won't hear it! And why the hell are you calling me Slim?"

"Because you're skinny like a beanpole… Slim."

Stone rushed toward the argument, his anxiety easing by a fraction. The sight would have been comical if not for Lisa's blood-soaked ACUs, her anger the result of Dillan dragging her by the rescue-strap of her tactical vest. The fingers of her right hand clawed the ground as her Sig, duct-taped to her left hand, bounced along at her side.

Stone joined them as Dillan lowered the pickup's gate. Without a word, he bent to help Dillan lift Lisa into the pickup's bed. Resignation setting in as the men tasked with transporting the wounded strapped her down, Lisa stared at Dillan, her grimy hand grasping his tightly.

"I love you, Slim."

"I love you too. And please, whatever you do, don't crawl out of the truck. We've got this under control."

She nodded as Dillan released her hand and slammed the gate. He watched the truck until it rounded the corner, disappearing from sight.

Dillan turned to face Stone, then quickly wrapped him in his arms. "It's good to see you. Please tell me you're not alone."

"We all made it, Dillan. It was close, but we lived."

"Was that Otto?" Randy's frantic voice startled both men.

"Jesus, Randy. You scared the living shit out of me," barked Dillan. "No, Otto was in the first Hummer. He should already be at the clinic."

Stone stiffened at Dillan's words. "Why is Otto going to the clinic?"

"Because he's a bullheaded fool who's forgotten that he's an old man," Randy shot back.

Stone, ignoring the truth in Randy's statement, bolted for the clinic, the sound of Randy's boots slapping the pavement close behind.

"Randy, where are Kit and Darline… where's everyone? Is our family safe?"

Randy caught up to Stone as they rounded the corner, bringing the clinic into view. "Kit and Darline are defending the north barrier. Natalia's taking care of resupply. Nila is at the east gate helping with first aid. Jack and Pat are outside the gate in the dump truck." He paused a long second before continuing, "Stone, we lost people today. We may lose more."

Stone slammed to a stop. "Who, who did we lose?"

Randy stammered, trying to remember the names of the friends lost to the sniper's scope. Stone waved him off. "No time. I need to see my brother," he said before continuing the race to the clinic.

Their pace quickened as they reached the clinic's tree-covered lawn. The sudden hiss of air-brakes pulled their attention to the International 4300 coming to a stop and blocking the clinic's driveway. The truck was an intimidating sight. Its improvised armor appeared medieval as the blood of its victims pooled on the pavement.

Stone didn't notice Jackson behind the killing machine's wheel and restarted his trek towards the clinic. Randy split off and charged towards the truck, intent on telling Jackson that they had found Otto.

His steps slowed as a third form came into view. Instinct pushed his hand to the 9mm holstered to his side.

"Who's that?" Randy asked, pointing at McCune.

Pat swung open her door while answering, "Relax, it's Doctor McCune. He's here to help with our wounded."

Eyes wide, Randy blurted, "Otto's in the clinic. So is Lisa. Both took a beating. Get the doctor in there. NOW."

Jackson rocketed from the truck's cab and bolted to the clinic, leaving McCune and Pat behind. The sights and sounds greeting Jackson inside the clinic were that of a battlefield hospital. Durrell and Sabrina barked orders to the volunteers helping with the wounded.

Pushed aside by Pat as she led McCune into the clinic, Jackson launched into a string of questions about his brother, all of which were overridden by Pat's single statement.

"Take the doctor to where he's needed most."

Sabrina grabbed the doctor by his arm and rushed him down a hallway. Jackson glanced around the room, searching for his brothers.

Durrell found Jackson's worried eyes and said, "Follow Sabrina. She'll take you to Otto and Stone. Then get back here. We need help. And bring Stone with you."

Randy hot on his heels, Jackson traversed the narrow hall. His search ended as the sounds of bickering voices pulled his attention to a room at the end of the hallway.

"Well, sounds like we found him and Lisa," Randy said over Jackson's shoulder.

A smile broke on Jackson's face. "Putting them in the same room wasn't Sabrina's best move."

As they inched closer, McCune's voice, similar to Jackson's father being asked, "Are we there yet," one too many times, rose above the others. "I will determine which of you sustained the worst injury. At that point, I will take the appropriate action to *fix this shit*, as you so eloquently articulated, Mister Hammer."

Stone's voice followed McCune's. "Otto, Lisa, let the doctor work. Seriously, your competition to prove yourselves the *best martyr ever* is annoying."

Jackson's smile grew. Judging by Stone's statement, the two were as ornery as ever. More importantly, they were alive.

His gut clenched as he entered the room and found his brother bare-chested and covered in blood from his waist down. McCune was hovering over him, examining a ragged gash on Otto's side. The doctor pressed on the area around the wound, causing Otto's left arm to shoot into the air, exposing a stark-white bandage soaked deep red down the middle.

Jackson and Stone moved as one to intercept their brother's attack on the doctor, but Sabrina cut them off. "Get out, now.

We've got this under control. That's the third time he's done that; he's not going to hit anyone. He's just a little soft when it comes to pain."

"Yeah, on your way, boys, your brother's a sissy. Nothing to see here," Lisa snipped from her bed.

Attention drawn to Lisa, the brothers noticed her damaged shoulder for the first time. Her color was awful, ghost-like, and her eyelids appeared to be losing the battle against gravity.

Jackson's head went back and forth between the two. Gulping air, he said, "Lisa needs to be first with... whatever it is you're doing, do it to her first."

"Nice, Jackson...." Otto spat before being cut off.

"Thank you, sir. I'll take your proposal under consideration. But for now, please follow Sabrina's direction and vacate the room," McCune said calmly but with enough force to pull Jackson's attention away from Otto.

Stone grasped Jackson's forearm and pulled him from the room. In the hall, they found a pallid, sweaty Randy leaning against the wall. "Is he... um, are they going to live?"

"You look worse than they do, Randy. You going to make it?"

"So much blood, and the doctor pushing around his side. But when I saw Lisa's shoulder, I got a bit woozy. I'm better now." After a long pause, Randy continued, "I think I need to sit down."

Stone and Jackson grabbed hold of Randy as McCune ordered Sabrina to prep for surgery.

CHAPTER 27 – DEEP CUTS

"Whoa! *Prep for surgery?* I'm thinking a few stitches, and I'm on my way. Maybe a transfusion. Add in six or seven days of bed rest. But surgery seems a little… drastic. Actually, a lot drastic."

I couldn't be certain, but McCune may have rolled his eyes before responding, "Mister Hammer, you will not require surgery. Although quite bloody, the injury itself is moderately superficial. The weapon missed any vital areas as it sliced through your *love handles*. You're a lucky man."

"Love handles?" My statement was barely audible over Lisa's cackling laughter. "Where'd you get your medical degree? I took a lot of damage, Doc. I mean, how do you explain the passing out, all the blood, or my disorientation?"

"Mister Hammer, as I stated, you lost a great deal of blood. That fact, coupled with your age and physical exertion, are the contributing factors to the symptoms you experienced. So I'm taking your brother's advice and working on Lisa first. We'll suture and bandage your wound and get back to you."

Lisa, though weak and whiter than the bedsheets she laid upon, was crying from laughter. She attempted to speak but only snorted through her hysterics.

"Why are you laughing, Lisa?" I snapped. "You're about to get cut, deep, by a person you've never met. Are you sure he's even a doctor?"

Sabrina, watching the exchange, quickly interjected, "Otto Hammer, why on earth would you say that?"

"Well, Sabrina, she started it."

With a shake of her head, she dismissed my defense as she wheeled a cart full of sharp medical instruments to Lisa's bedside.

Lisa went quiet at the sight of the IV bag, or more accurately, the needle.

"Hey," I began, "when did we get IV stuff? Are you going to operate on her while she's awake?" My statement caused Lisa to go a shade whiter.

"Never thought about that, did ya, Lisa? They'll probably give you some whiskey and a block of wood to bite on. It's how they did it in the Old West."

McCune moved between Lisa and me. He bent down and whispered in my ear, "If you don't stop, I'll use a rusty ten-penny nail to suture your wound." Pivoting to Lisa before I could respond, he continued, "Lisa, please ignore Otto. He's lost a lot of blood and, as a result, his cognitive abilities are suffering. You will be sedated for the procedure, with a proper anesthetic administered by a trained professional." A smile as warm as the sun creased his features. "You're in capable hands. We're going to ensure no bullet fragments remain, then we'll repair that clavicle. You're a lucky young lady. A few inches lower, and this conversation would have been much more complicated."

McCune spun and locked me in a challenging stare. Message received. I kept my mouth shut.

Craning my neck to get eyes on Lisa, I found a warrior staring stoically back at me as Sabrina slid the catheter needle into her forearm. "Hey, you got this. The doctor passed my test. I'll be here when you wake up."

Lisa tilted her head and had time to smile before the medicine worked its magic.

***

With Stone and Jackson's help, Sabrina moved me to another room before beginning Lisa's surgery. The topical pain killer she administered took the edge off, but by no means had my pain fully subsided. While I enlightened everyone as to my level of pain, Stone, unceremoniously, deposited me on a freshly made, single-sized bed.

"What the hell! Are you trying to kill me? They need some gurneys in this place. Or, at a minimum, competent orderlies."

Stone, face palming, answered, "The doctor said you'll live. Actually, he said, your wound is *moderately superficial*. Thank God for your *love handles*. And, if you paid attention, they have gurneys. They reserve them for the serious patients. Not their patients with *superficial injuries*."

Air pumped through my flared nostrils as I locked Stone in a withering stare. The mother of all retorts perched on the tip of my tongue when a feminine voice broke through. "Otto Hammer, I should… how could you… why did you do that?" Darline stammered, voice vacillating between anger and relief.

My epic response to Stone vanished at the sight of my wife. Her eyes, filled with concern, pierced mine. She pushed past my brothers and knelt at my side. Her eyes getting watery, she tilted her head as a single tear raced down her cheek.

"I'm using every ounce of energy to stop myself from beating you unconscious, Otto Hammer." The sincerity in her words was off-putting and caused me to cover my face in case she lost her battle with self-control.

"It's good to see you too, babe," I said from behind my forearms. "I have to say, I'm feeling the love of my family right now. It's a warm, glowing love which fills me with joy."

Risking a peek from behind my protective barrier, I found her smiling face. I reached out and pulled her into an embrace. "I'm sorry," I whispered, "It just happened. I saw Devon's blood…" I stopped cold. "Where's Devon?"

Metal clanging on metal broke my thought as Durrell pushed a medical cart into the crowded room. "Devon's fine. Scared to death, sporting five stitches and an eye that has swollen shut, but all told, he's good. His aunt is with him until we can get Tesha here."

Stone stepped from the room while talking over his shoulder. "She's at the east gate. I'll go get her."

"How'd she do?"

Stone stopped at the threshold and turned to face me. "She's a natural. Had a slight issue with a double feed but worked through it while keeping her head in the fight."

"Who cleaned her gun?" I barked. "A clean gun is a reliable gun. If those shit-balls on the gun-cleaning team screwed this up… well, let's just say I'll be paying them a visit!"

"Relax, Otto. It was her husband's gun; she doesn't let anyone touch it. It was just one of those things." With that, he vanished into the hallway.

Darline's eyes went wide. I followed her stare to Durrell's cart. He had removed a white cloth which had been concealing its contents. The reason for Darline's reaction quickly came into focus.

Durrell was preparing to suture my wound, and his tray was crammed with what I can only describe as medieval torture devices.

His chuckle drew my attention to his smiling face. It was not a warm or friendly smile. It was the smile of a torturer who enjoys his work. "Mister Hammer, are you ready?" he asked as he held a large syringe with a blue ball where the plunger should have been. "We're going to start by irrigating that nasty *little* wound of yours. Gotta keep it from getting infected."

Darline, understanding what was happening in my brain after I noticed the needles, quickly leaned in and kissed my forehead. "I'm going down the hall, maybe check in on Devon, clean up some UC, anything but witness what's about to happen." Then, she whispered, "Please behave. He's trying to help."

As my wife led Randy and Jackson from the room, Durrell moved into position. Smile a bit more twisted, he said, "Tell me, Otto. Do you remember that time I asked to borrow a quarter-inch socket wrench because mine had broken in the middle of working on my car's alternator?"

I shook my head because I honestly didn't remember.

"Ah, well, let me refresh you. It was roughly one hundred degrees that day. I had worked a double shift when my car died on the way home. Actually, at the end of the street. I mean, I could see my house, but my car wouldn't move another inch. *Randy* drove by, offered me a ride to Auto Zone then to my house, so I could change and get my tools. He couldn't stay to help because he was picking Nila up from work. Randy sure is a nice guy." He paused, making a show of filling the syringe with pure rubbing alcohol.

"Yeah, that was one miserable day. Hot and humid, so humid that my knuckles were bloody from slipping off of my wrench. That's how the driver ended up damaged. The third time I slammed my knuckles on the alternator's bracket, I smashed it on the pavement. It wouldn't lock after that."

"Sounds like you owned some cheap tools," I blurted out in a feeble attempt at lightening the mood.

Durrell's head cocked to the side. "It belonged to my dad, passed down from my grandfather."

"Oh, well then, it was probably old and fragile." I was flailing.

"Old yes, fragile, not so much. Anyway, I saw you mowing your lawn. Moseyed on down to ask a neighbor for help, actually, not even help, just a tool... to simply borrow a tool. Do you know what you said?"

I knew what I'd said. I didn't remember him asking, but I knew what my answer was.

"No. Just no. Not *hey, I don't have one* or *can't let you borrow it, but I'll help*. Nope, you just said no. At that moment, I understood why people think you're a jerk, Otto."

"This is going to hurt, isn't it?" I asked as he moved in with the syringe.

"Oh, it's going to hurt *so* much. Although not nearly as bad as the stitches. Seems I misplaced my curved suturing needle. I'll be using a sewing needle for this one." He chuckled, then plunged the irrigator into my side and forced the alcohol into my body.

Darline burst into the room, drawn by my anguished cries for help. The urgency left her body as she realized I wasn't dying. Sweat poured down my face while Durrell exacted his revenge. I struggled to remain still as the needle made its first pass through my skin. Darline went pale, pivoted, and left the room as quickly as she'd entered.

"I'm not good with needles. Durrell, can't you spray some of that topical stuff on it, like Sabrina did?"

"Oh, I'm sorry, Otto. Is this uncomfortable? I wonder if the beating my knuckles took that day damaged some nerves, making my hands unsteady."

"Come on, man. That was a long time ago. Hell, I don't even remember you asking. Plus, you said it yourself. Everyone thinks I'm a jerk. You should have known I wouldn't let you borrow my tools. I don't let anyone borrow my tools, not even Darline."

Defending my actions only egged him on. He held up his hand holding the needle for my viewing pleasure and made sure I saw it trembling as it disappeared from sight, headed for my side.

After what felt like two hours, he knotted and snipped. "All finished, Mister Hammer. Please be sure to leave positive feedback when you complete our customer satisfaction survey."

He pushed back from my bedside while removing his gloves as Sabrina entered the room. "Prep for surgery, Durrell; we're getting overwhelmed."

Durrell grabbed an IV bag, flipped my hand palm down, and jabbed a pencil-sized needle into the first vein he saw. Taking a more serious tone, he said, "I'm giving you antibiotics. You're going to be here a while. Get comfortable." He rushed from the room.

CHAPTER 28 – PULL THE TRIGGER

The drone's video feed showed a world unlike any Willis had imagined possible. San Francisco appeared a wasteland. Smoke billowed from flame-engulfed buildings as trash mingled with the dead on the streets of the once beautiful city. Landmarks which, a few short months ago topped his bucket list of places to visit, stood in ruins.

The RQ-4 drone banked hard toward San Francisco Bay, crossing mere feet over the Oakland Bay Bridge. Gridlocked cars sat abandoned on the monstrous structure's deck, the bloody remnants of their former occupants revealed as thousands of enraged scavenger birds took flight when the drone interrupted their feeding frenzy.

Its flight path took it up the coast as it scouted for enemy landing parties that may have split from the main DPRK force. It found only death and broadcast those images to Fort Riley's TOC.

The TOC went still as battle-hardened soldiers stared in disbelief at the carnage. Suddenly, the image fluttered before being replaced by video of a small city surrounded by a desert landscape.

A voice broadcast over the TOC's speakers clarified what they were seeing as the drone's camera zoomed in. "This is Wendover, Utah, bordering Nevada in the Great Salt Lake Desert. During the mission, one of our C130s experienced a malfunction with its antidote delivery system over Alameda. During its flight to refuel at Hill Air Force Base, the malfunction corrected and released hundreds of gallons of the antidote over Wendover. The results are obvious."

The video feed showed a confused population as dozens of people wandered the streets aimlessly. Suddenly, the video seemed to magnify, bringing the images into sharper focus.

The video locked onto a small group in tattered clothing, heading toward a small flat-roofed structure roughly three hundred yards south of Interstate 80.

"This city was void of life less than forty-eight hours ago. Obviously, that is no longer the case."

McMaster, standing between his son and Willis, whispered, "Get ready, boys. You're about to go weapons hot." Both men nodded their agreement with the elder McMaster's statement.

The voice of Chairman Mallet again filled the TOC. "Infrared scans indicate we have living humans in this city. Ones, which only days ago, were UCs." After an effectual pause, Mallet continued, "We plan to make contact with these people, determine if they are free of the virus, and extract them if they are. Eight hours have passed since we dispersed the antidote on Wendover. We have not witnessed the violent reaction befalling North Korea's invasion force. Ladies and gentlemen, these people may hold the answer to crush the virus."

The room bristled with excitement, sweeping everyone into the moment.

"Colonel Stein, assemble an expeditionary force. You will make contact ASAP. Questions?"

Stein visually surveyed the room. Met with grim determination, he responded, "The Big Red One is clear. We will have boots on the ground in three hours."

Obviously smiling as he spoke, Mallet said, "That's why we called the Big Red One. Godspeed, soldiers."

McMaster was barking orders the instant the broadcast ended. "Willis, Nathan, kit-up. Be battle ready in ten."

The men were moving before McMaster finished, Willis trailing Nathan as they headed for the armory.

"What's our force strength?" Willis asked while at a full run.

"I'm thinking a six-person fire-team, but I'm confident Sergeant Major has other plans. Whatever they are, you can trust him. His instincts are solid."

Struggling to keep pace with Nathan, Willis huffed through his response. "I've been in his office and seen the citations. Enough said."

Nathan and Willis, in full battle-rattle, burst through the door of the TOC exactly ten minutes later. They found Sergeant Major McMaster engaged in a hushed conversation with Colonel Stein, its seriousness telegraphed by the hard stare McMaster had the younger but higher-ranking Stein locked in.

When the colonel finally smiled and shook his head, Nathan leaned in close to Willis and whispered, "Sergeant Major McMaster just won whatever argument they were having."

The colonel acknowledged the young warfighters and stepped away from McMaster, taking a position in front of an enormous monitor displaying drone footage of the desolate city of Wendover.

"Jennings will be here momentarily. I have assigned Lange and Watts to your fire-team. Willis will be team lead," McMaster said as the soldiers rumbled into the TOC, shouldering up to Willis and Nathan. A split second later, Jennings joined them in front of the TOC's monitor.

Willis noticed the crisp way with which McMaster rolled through the mission plan. He understood that the sergeant major was visualizing the battlefield and working through several contingency plans should his main battleplan go sideways.

The confidence he displayed made it sound like a simple extraction. Jennings would drop them on Interstate 80. They would traverse the fencing, make a beeline to the flat-topped building—now identified as a motel—locate the group, administer the virus test, assess their condition, and rally at the Black Hawk for exfiltration. The Black Hawk would recon the city to their south, drawing any UCs away from the team. Her M134 would be onsite in seconds if needed.

McMaster stiffened his back and met each of their stares. The glint in his eyes spoke to his pride in seeing the best warfighters RAM had to offer standing in front of him. He asked one question: "Understood?"

"Hooah, sir," was the team's unanimous reply.

McMaster dismissed them with a stiff nod. "We'll have a drone overhead, and you'll have direct communications to the TOC. I will see *all* of you in ten hours."

***

Jennings flared the Hawk left, then leveled out. Before beginning her descent, she opened coms. "Gentlemen, and I use that term loosely, your call-sign is Dorothy. Sergeant Willis is Dorothy Actual. My call-sign remains Wicked One. Be mindful of the relationship between Dorothy and the Wicked Witch when communicating with me."

Willis gave Nathan a quizzical look and received a broad smile in return. "Yes, ma'am, I mean Miss Wicked One. We will mind our manners when communicating with Her Royal Highness," Nathan quipped, eliciting some much-needed laughter from the team.

Willis leaned in close to Nathan and covered his helmet's boom mic. "You ready for this?"

"Sergeant Willis, I fought my way from LA to the Utah border with a baseball bat. I'm most assuredly ready for this."

"Hooah," Willis replied with a smile.

Dust whipped into the Black Hawk's cabin, reminding Willis of his last mission in the sandbox—thankfully minus the rattle of enemy AK47s. He was lost in the moment until the firm grip of Nathan's hand on his shoulder urged him to disembark.

Boots on pavement a flash later, Willis went to a knee to cover the others spilling from the warbird. A quick glance over his shoulder confirmed that the four-man team was ready. "Let's move," he screamed over the powerful engine of the Black Hawk as it ascended, then roared away to recon and decoy the dead.

The four operators sprinted down an embankment towards the fence separating I-80 from the city of Wendover. From their vantage point, the city appeared abandoned, but the idyllic scene hadn't fooled them.

Corporal Lange cut an access hole in the fence in thirty seconds. Following the battle plan, Watts took point as he pushed through the opening. The team fell into a wedge formation behind him and slowed their pace as they crossed the three hundred yards of flat, hard-packed earth.

Willis halted the team thirty yards from the target structure and had them form up around him. "We locate the survivors, evaluate their condition, and bug out. Clear?"

As the team confirmed their understanding, they heard a garbled cry for help. They went still, waiting for it to repeat. It did. A grime-streaked face came into view, framed by an open window in the building thirty yards west of their position.

Willis was moving an instant later, taking point as he heel-toed his way toward the survivor. Halfway to the window, it became clear something was wrong. The person in the window barely resembled a human, let alone one that was alive and healthy.

When the survivor noticed Willis approaching, it emitted a sound resembling the cry of a wounded animal. Willis stopped mid-step, shouldered his M4, and placed its red dot on the pathetic being's forehead.

"Sergeant Willis, what the hell was that?" Nathan barked.

"I think it came from the person in the window. Cover our flanks; I'm going to verify."

Lang and Watts took up positions covering the team's flanks, while Nathan turned to cover their six. Willis was three feet from the window when he pulled to a stop.

The film-covered eyes staring at him sent a chill through the battle-hardened warrior. Festering wounds covered skin stained blue by the antidote and emitted a stench so foul Willis gagged and pulled his shemagh over his nose.

"I'm Sergeant Willis, Right America military. Identify yourself."

Two equally damaged faces suddenly appeared in the background as the first answered Willis. "Please help. Need help. Monsters eat." Its voice sounded as if it was speaking through a mouth full of marbles.

The childlike response set Willis on edge. He restarted his approach when suddenly the face disappeared from view. The action stopped Willis; gripped by indecision, he took a cautious step toward the window.

"Sergeant Wills, whatever you're doing, do it quickly. We have hostiles to our north."

"Living or dead?" Willis asked.

Lang delayed his response as he scanned the area through his rifle scope. "A little of both."

Willis snapped in Lang's direction. "Clarify."

"They are definitely UCs, but they appear to be tracking us, using cover, staggering their movements. I'm counting twenty-five to thirty."

Willis pivoted back to the window. A different pair of hazy eyes stared back at him. The pathetic being attempted to speak but only managed that horrible noise they'd heard moments earlier.

"Nathan, you're with me. Lang, Watts, hold the line. We're going to make contact with the survivors, assess their condition, and determine if they are a threat. Engage hostiles approaching your position."

Nathan followed Willis as they sprinted towards the corner of the building. Willis recalled the drone image of the building and determined the path he was taking was the quickest route to the front of the structure. The survivors' location should be three doors from this side of the building.

Willis signaled a stop and took a knee positioned at the front corner leading to the building's parking lot. The next turn would take them to the room holding the survivors. He leaned out and scanned the area. What he saw was jolting. "Nathan, I'm not sure what's happening. But it doesn't look like a cure. Let's move."

The warriors broke from cover and bolted towards their target. Understanding washed over Nathan when the area came into view. Bodies littered the parking lot. Blood, trickling from ghastly wounds, glistened in the sun, showed they were freshly dead bodies. *What the...*

Nathan's thought broke as Willis kicked the door from its hinges. M4s shouldered, the soldiers rushed into a room thick with the putrid stench of decay. Weapon-mounted flashlights cut through the dank gloom, searching for the survivors but finding only death.

Three bodies lay side-by-side atop a shabby queen-sized bed. Weeks-old blood, now the color of tar, stained pillows under heads destroyed by a single bullet.

"Murder-suicide?" asked Nathan.

Otto inspected the remains as the scene played out in his mind's eye. "Dad killed the child, his wife, then himself. I shudder to think how many times this scenario played out across our country."

Their reverence shattered as the bathroom door shook violently, snapping the men back to reality. "Identify yourself," Willis barked.

Receiving only the pitiable cry of a wounded animal in response, Willis stepped towards the door, preparing to breach it. It burst open, spilling three damaged forms into the room. Willis slid his finger to the trigger of his M4 as they rushed his position.

"Stop!" Willis shouted.

To his surprise, they did. Then one of them attempted to communicate while whirling its hands frantically and screeching and hissing.

Willis stared in disbelief. These people had been dead, been UCs, mere days ago—their blood-stained clothing a testament to violence unleashed upon them. Gore-matted faces told the story of the atrocities they'd committed after they had turned.

Willis realized what he needed to do and pulled the trigger.

CHAPTER 29 – NEGATIVE

"Shots fired!" Nathan yelled into his boom mic as he crossed the room.

"SITREP?" McMaster's voice boomed through Willis' headset.

"Sergeant Major, this is Dorothy Actual. The survivors are a negative. We will secure a body for further inspection at Fort Riley, over."

"Sergeant Willis, I need a situation report ASAP."

Nathan had reached Willis' side and stared down at the bodies. He'd been guarding their six and had caught only snippets of Willis' interaction with them. But he was no longer confused by his team leader's action.

What lay before him were shells of human beings. Deformed and brutalized. Their first contact with the group had put Nathan on edge. He'd known something was terribly wrong; his instincts told him it would end badly, and it did. Seeing them up close confirmed his suspicions. Blue-tinted pus ran freely from festering wounds. Skin swelled then popped, spewing more of the wretched-smelling liquid from their lifeless bodies. The action reminded him of a bubbling caldron from a long-forgotten fairytale.

Willis glanced at Nathan and received a confirming nod. "Sergeant Major, this is Dorothy Actual. The antidote is a failure. These people were no longer functioning humans…"

Three voices battling for his attention filled his radio, cutting off his transmission. Of the three, Lang's voice rose above the others. "Hostiles closing fast."

Willis regained control of the conversation, shouting down the competing voices to reach his team. "Lang, Watts, open fire. Wicked One, this is Dorothy Actual requesting fire support, over."

"Dorothy Actual, Wicked One is en route, out."

Nathan bolted towards the door as Willis gave the order to join Lang and Watts behind the motel. Willis caught up to him an instant later, and the warriors double-timed to support their teammates.

As the pair rounded the corner, M4s screamed to life, cutting down the leading edge of the UC mob. The thumping sensation deep in his chest told Willis that Wicked One would be on scene soon. An instant later, the purr of an M134 Minigun filled the air as the earth exploded through the UC ranks. Bodies vaulted skyward as thousands of heavy rounds slammed into putrid flesh.

Willis' team was safe, for now. It was time to secure one of the blue monsters he had killed inside the motel. "Nathan, you're with me. Lang, Watts, link up with Wicked One. We will rally in five. Wicked One, remain in position."

Three minutes later, Willis and Nathan were dragging a blue-stained bedsheet around the building and prepared to rally with Wicked One when McMaster's voice buzzed in Willis' ear. "Dorothy Actual, SITREP."

"Sergeant Major, we have secured a body for testing. Preparing to EXFIL. No casualties to report. Please tell me the drone recorded the UC attacking our team, over."

A new voice burst into Willis' speaker. "Dorothy Actual, this is Chairman Mallet. Do not, under any circumstances, transport that body to Fort Riley. Check your uniforms for any sign of a blue liquid. If found, discard the contaminated clothing ASAP." Mallet paused, then with a strained voice, said, "Soldier. If the liquid contacted your skin, I'm ordering you to remain in Wendover. That order holds for your entire team."

Willis and Nathan's gloved hands released their grip on the bedsheet. Willis glanced at the shattered, bloody bodies strewn about the battlefield in front of him as Wicked One began her descent, swirling debris into the air. Eyes wide, he screamed into his mic, "Wicked One, pull off! Abort landing. Proceed to our original LZ."

He matched his team's questioning gazes as the Hawk sped away. "That blue shit is everywhere. The last thing we need is the Hawk's rotor-wash spraying it all over us."

Lang and Watts, standing at the edge of the slaughter, moved to distance themselves from the deadly liquid as Willis barked orders: "Move to the LZ. Once there, inspect yourself for any sign of the liquid. Remove your clothing... you know what, when we reach the LZ, just strip to your skivvies and inspect each other."

On the move before he finished speaking, the team discarded their ACUs as they ran. It would have been comical if not for the reason driving their actions. The team, now wearing only their pants, gloves, helmets, and boots, arrived at the Landing Zone as the warbird touched down. Rifles clattered to the ground as each man stripped, but Willis stopped before getting his pants off.

Nathan locked him in a hard stare. "How'd it happen?"

Willis turned sideways, sticking a finger into a ragged tear in his pants just above his ankle. "Don't know how it happened, and that's not important now," he said as he removed his gloved finger, blue dye staining its tip.

"Son of a bitch! Look, you're coming back with us. We can isolate you."

Willis waved Nathan off. "You know I can't. Load up. Now, soldier."

Nathan growled, "Lang, Watts, give Sergeant Willis your rifles." He paused as the men scooped up their weapons and handed them to Willis. "Our packs have some food in them, and our camelbacks are full." He nodded to the deserted items marking their path. "You'll be good for a couple of days. We're coming back for you!"

Resignation setting in, Willis collected the team's supplies as he made his way towards the motel. When the roar of the Black Hawk faded, he lowered his boom mic and hailed Riley's TOC, "Dorothy Actual for Sergeant Major McMaster, over."

Static bounced around his speaker before McMaster replied, "Go for McMaster, over."

"Sir, I need to talk to Camp Hopkins, Chief Albright, over."

"We can do that. And Willis, I'm sorry."

Fifteen minutes later, as Willis barricaded himself into a corner room of the motel, affording forward-, east-, and rear-facing lines-of-sight, Albright's voice broke over the radio, "Albright for Sergeant Willis, over."

"Sir, I need to speak to my family. Can you make that happen? Over."

"Give me ten. They stopped the attack on the community. They're assessing casualties; we'll get Lucas on coms and have her corral your family, over."

"Thank you, and thanks for the update. Ask her to find that pain in the ass, Otto, too, over."

"Understood. And Willis, we will see you again. Have I been clear? Over."

Willis' chin went to rest on his chest. "I'll talk to you in ten. Willis, out."

CHAPTER 30 – WAR ROOM

Flocci answered his phone without bothering to check caller ID. "Where have you been? I called you two days ago. Do you understand what's happening? How close we are?"

"Close to what, Doctor?"

Flocci pulled a sharp breath. "Mister President, I apologize. I was expecting an update from… from Doctor McCune."

"Oh, McCune, you say. How is the good doctor? He's a good man, one of the best, actually. One of the greatest RAM citizens to ever live." Train paused, a grin forming on his face. "So, tell me, Doctor, how's the Alameda test going? Any progress in that area, you know, curing the virus?"

Eyes shifting wildly, Flocci paced the length of his office. "Mister President, I'm afraid I have discouraging news. It seems McCune isn't the man we thought he was. We've found flaws in his work, deadly flaws. When confronted with the science, he disappeared."

"Disappeared, you say. Just vanished? Huh, seems a mighty achievement for an unarmed man with zero military training to slip away these days, what with all the monsters running loose. Explain."

Sweat beaded on Flocci's forehead. A feeling he was unaccustomed to began taking root: panic! "We here at the CDC share your disbelief. And the information I'm about to divulge left us utterly astounded. I requested he relocate to the CDC facility to further assist in his research. When our team arrived to escort him, they found he'd gone missing. An investigation quickly ensued, and we discovered… sir, please brace yourself. McCune has been conspiring with Russian operatives."

He couldn't be sure, but he thought he detected Train's muffled laugh before he spoke. "Ohhhh, the Russians? Terrible people, just terrible. Can't trust them. You may recall I'm very familiar with how they work. I'm curious—how did you determine McCune was working with Russian operatives? I would have guessed North Korea as the main enemy player."

Flocci went red at his misstep. "Um, I do, sir. It was a viciously turbulent time in our country's history. To answer your question… I can't, I can't answer it because you already know what's happening, you worthless windbag."

Train responded through clenched teeth, "You knew the antidote wasn't ready. Why did the test move forward? What were you promised, and by whom?"

Flocci screwed his eyes shut as the sound of boots slapping against marble tiles reached him. The muffled objections from his security detail were quickly shouted down by what he assumed were well-armed soldiers here to whisk him away to some government-controlled Black Site.

With nothing to lose, Flocci began answering the president's questions. "Think about it, Train. I held the power to end life on this planet. I simply needed to show the world who was in control. World leaders would bow at my feet. Beg to be spared from the destruction. Pay any amount to find themselves in my good graces. We can still…"

Suddenly his office door exploded. Shards of polished oak hurtled towards his face as he sought an escape route from his expansive office. A soldier threw Flocci to the ground, ending his rant. Still clutching his phone, he caught one last comment from Train. "*Primum non nocere*, Doctor. First, do no harm."

Train disconnected the call and swiveled his chair to face the monitor on the wall. The War Room, deep inside Cheyenne Mountain, remained in stunned silence. Nothing had changed. The monitor cycled between video feeds of Alameda, California, and Wendover, Utah. Each feed broadcast the same story. The antidote had failed.

Thousands of people appeared cured of the virus, only to die as the antidote reached maximum saturation in their systems. Some simply bled out from old wounds sustained during their life as a UC; others dropped for no apparent reason while large pustules formed on their skin, then burst. But those weren't the monsters responsible for shocking the battle-hardened military men and women to silence. That honor belonged to the beasts now referred to as Blue Savages.

They were spotted moments before boots hit the ground in Wendover. Seconds later, all watching realized the antidote had created monsters far more lethal than the ones they had been fighting. Mallet watched, horrified, as they quickly formed hunting packs and performed what appeared to be door-to-door searches for the living. Humans, temporarily cured by the antidote, were flushed out, torn to shreds, and devoured.

Mallet pulled a sharp breath when the Blue Savages herded the less-developed UCs together and used them as decoys to ensnare the cured. The Blue Savages eviscerated those UCs unable to aid in the slaughter. At that point, he realized he needed to pull the team out of Wendover. He was two minutes too late.

Train stared across the table at the Joint Chiefs. Shifting his gaze to Mallet, he said, "What's the plan?"

"Mister President, I have no idea. This level of intelligence is something we've not encountered."

Train leaned forward, preparing to respond, when one of the dozens of analysts seated at an equal number of monitors spoke: "Savage Blues are collapsing."

Mallet, thankful for the intrusion, pivoted towards the young woman. "Clarify."

"Sir, it just started; they're dropping like dominos in Alameda. Once down, they don't attempt to stand. Actually, they don't move at all. They appear... dead."

A second analyst spoke up. "I can confirm the same in Wendover."

Now standing, Mallet asked, "Anyone have a theory? Have we secured McCune's notes? Do we know his location?"

Silence greeted Mallet. He understood. The world was still attempting to wrap its collective head around dead people eating the living. How could he expect them to run down this rabbit hole?

"Understood," Mallet said, acknowledging the ridiculousness of his first question. "Do we have a lead on McCune?"

A man, sitting in a darkened corner, responded. "Sir, I have Camp Hopkins on my secured line. They have information on McCune."

"Patch them through. NOW."

CHAPTER 31 – A PROMISE MADE

It startled Albright when Chairman Mallet's voice issued from the speaker in Camp Hopkins' Tactical Operation Center. He went cold when the President's voice followed. When he informed the analyst what had happened at Camp Hopkins, he'd had no idea of the implications.

"Chief Warrant Officer Albright. We understand you may possess information regarding the whereabouts of Doctor McCune."

"Sir, to clarify. I have information regarding members of the CDC arriving, unannounced, via a C130 delivering medical supplies to Camp Hopkins. They commandeered a Humvee and set out as quickly as they arrived. No mention of McCune. But sir, I have a question. President Train's signature was on the orders they produced. Shouldn't you already be aware of their reason for being here?"

Train slammed a hand on the conference table. "That son of a bitch! How many other orders has he presented in my name?"

Albright raged at the realization. "Mister President, the papers they produced appeared legitimate. My apologies for the oversight. I promise you, we will deal with them when they return."

"Albright," Mallet began, "to be clear. They haven't returned with the doctor?"

"Not that I'm aware of. We've been preoccupied defending against an attack on a local community. Sir, what's going on?"

A young soldier, Corporal Offutt, who'd been monitoring the radio traffic from the Black Hawk mopping up the attack on Otto's community, interrupted Albright's conversation. "Chief, our air assets located an abandoned Humvee two klicks north of the community."

Two things happened simultaneously. Mallet, overhearing the information, reacted exactly the way Albright had expected by ordering a search of the area. And the TOC's administrative specialist announced that he had made contact with Lucas.

Two birds, one stone, thought Albright. "Patch her through to primary coms." He then shifted his attention to Offutt. "Order them to smoke the Humvee's location."

Lucas was on speaker an instant later.

"Lucas, I want your Bradley on that smoke ASAP. Clear the area and locate three people. Two military and one civilian VIP. Assume military as hostile and engage if necessary. Do NOT harm the VIP."

Albright could hear Lucas as she repeated his orders, verbatim, to her team. When she finished, Albright immediately spoke. "Lucas, are you with Sergeant Willis' family?"

"Affirmative on Willis' family. Sir, why are they here? Is Willis...?" Her silence was deafening.

"Sergeant, it's important that I speak with them at the same time. Give them each a helmet. After I'm done speaking with them, I'll need you to do the same for Otto."

The sound of rustling fabric preceded the fear-strained voices of Logan and Addie as they confirmed they were both present.

"Logan, Addie, I'm patching you through to your brother. Hold tight."

Counting the IV drips, I'd started dozing off when the red-eyed monster poked her head into the room.

"Hey, Otto, how ya feeling?"

"Well now, that depends. Are you going to take advantage of my weakened condition and slap me around? Or is this an actual wellbeing check?"

No bluster, no threats, and no name-calling; just red-rimmed, watery eyes staring at me.

"Sergeant Lucas, are you okay? You're kinda freaking me out."

"Otto, Willis wants to talk to you," she said while holding her helmet out for me. The lack of an insult about my head being too fat to fit into her helmet raised my anxiety level.

With a hard slap on top of the helmet, I got it to cover my ears. "Sergeant Willis, make this quick; Lucas' tiny helmet might squeeze my brain through my ears."

A soft chuckle filtered through the speaker, followed by my friend's voice. "Mister Otto, you just don't know when to keep your pie-hole shut, do you? Don't answer. I don't have a lot of time. I have information the community needs to act on."

I sat quietly while Willis shared the horrific news about the Blue Savages. My head went woozy when he told me about his team being stalked by a group of them. Then he leveled the worst of it. RAM had deployed an antidote, and it had failed in spectacular fashion.

"Willis, what are we talking about here? If these things go *Twenty-eight Days Later* on us, we're screwed."

"Otto, I have no idea what that means."

"Damn, Willis, have you ever even been to a movie theater? It's the movie where the zombies are super fast and aggressive. No shambling, mindless dolts; they're hardcore killers. Scary as hell."

Another soft laugh from Willis preceded his voice, one that sounded uncharacteristically subdued. "Nope, nothing like what you're describing. But they organized into a fighting unit, and they displayed more agility than we're used to." Silence thick enough to dull a knife's edge followed.

"Willis, what's going on? Anyone could have delivered this information and delivered it to someone far more stable than me. Spit it out, man."

I wished I had taken a deep breath when he spoke, but I hadn't, and I struggled to get air into my lungs. My vision went hazy as tears stung my eyes. Allowing my head to drop to the pillow, I stuffed my rage away to visit later.

"You're not coming home?" I asked through gasping breaths. His silent confirmation nearly crushed me.

When he finally spoke, he asked one thing of me: "Otto, keep my family safe."

"I will. I promise."

CHAPTER 32 – BLOOD TYPE

After Otto handed the radio back to Lucas, Albright waited a heartbeat before speaking. "Lucas, what's your twenty? Over."

"The infirmary, over."

"Perfect. You need to determine if someone named McCune is in that facility. He's a doctor, and the President needs to talk to him ASAP."

Lucas bolted from Otto's room, making a beeline for the small waiting area turned triage. She knew who she needed to find as she searched the faces of the people tending to the wounded. Her eyes locked onto Pat, and after making her way through the crowded space, she found herself caught in the matriarch's icy glare.

"Pat, I need to verify if a doctor named McCune is here."

"Who's asking?" Pat answered.

"Your answer tells me he's here. Where?"

Pat stared defiantly at the sergeant. They needed him. She wasn't about to turn him over to the same government that had tried to execute him.

Frustration bubbling over, Lucas barked, "Pat, the President wants to talk to him. I don't know why, but my guess is that McCune has important information regarding the virus."

Eyes still locked onto Lucas', Pat finally answered. "McCune, huh, never heard of him. Now, if you'll excuse me, I need to get back to helping my friends."

Lucas took a menacing step in Pat's direction.

Pat matched the move. "Take your best shot, Sergeant," she growled.

As Lucas contemplated her next move, a voice broke the stalemate. "Ladies, please, we've seen enough bloodshed today."

Lucas pivoted, preparing to belittle the intruder, but the man interrupted. "I'm Doctor McCune. If you're here on behalf of Doctor Flocci, I assure you I will not accompany you to the CDC."

Moments later, Doctor McCune sat with his face buried in his hands, struggling to control his anger. His stomach threatened to heave its meager contents to the floor. "The arrogant fool didn't listen to me. I warned him not to move forward with the test. You must believe me, Mister President, I tried to stop him."

"Doctor, we believe you. Plus, he confessed. Now tell us what we can expect from these monsters. How do we fight them? More importantly, how do we keep this variant from spreading?"

McCune pulled air deep into his lungs, trying to calm his quickly unraveling mind. After he felt he'd placed his nervous breakdown on hold, he addressed Train's questions. He moved through the information as if he were reading directly from his notes.

"It's all driven by blood type, sir. That's the determining factor in how the body responds to the antidote. Several outcomes are plausible, some less desirable than others. Our human trials found that living subjects with AB negative blood developed high levels of aggression. They killed for the sake of killing.

"If a subject had already succumbed to the virus, the result was an exceedingly aggressive, more mobile UC with higher cognitive skills than its predecessors. A super UC, if you will. The unknown is super UC to human transfer; my fear is it creates a hybrid monster evolving beyond our capabilities to contain it. To date, we have been unable to duplicate the exact circumstances responsible for our blood donor's success in fighting off the virus. The key lay in the entirety of his treatment after his exposure to the virus."

Pat, listening from just outside the slightly opened door to the room McCune sat in, pulled a sharp breath. *Super UCs; hybrids. Are you kidding me?* The thought promised to steal her sanity. She removed her pen and notepad from the inside pocket of her jacket and scribbled a note. Waving the paper in the air to get Darline's attention, she stuffed the note into her friend's hand, then turned her attention back to the conversation.

Darline exploded through the hospital's door at a full run, Pat's note clutched in her hand. She took a confirming glance. She hadn't misread it. *"Hide Andy!"* was written in her friend's flawless penmanship.

Pat grew frustrated with only being able to hear McCune's side of the conversation. She pushed the door open a smidge more, hoping to hear the full conversation. Lucas, sitting across from the doctor, noticed the movement and met Pat's fearful stare, then nodded her approval just as McCune resumed speaking.

"Sir, I'm afraid it will take years, many years, to develop a successful antidote. A vaccine appears unlikely. The human trials did not produce antibodies or any positive results in our test subjects other than curing several previously incurable diseases, most notably, cancer. It had no effect on humans outside the aforementioned blood types."

"Doctor, this is Chairman Mallet of the Joint Chiefs of Staff. How do we fight them? Do they have any exploitable weaknesses?"

McCune pondered the question before speaking. "Yes, they do. Time. As you've likely witnessed, their lifespan is quite limited. Once the antidote reaches maximum saturation, their death-clock begins ticking, and internal decay accelerates. Uninfected persons with AB negative blood burn out rather quickly; a matter of hours defines their post antidote lifespan. Infected subjects can wreak havoc for longer, possibly forty-eight hours. I haven't performed an in-depth analysis of their life-cycle, but their slowed metabolic rate would dictate a longer, but not indefinite, life cycle. I'm basing that estimation on the early studies of the antidote on our infected subjects. Again, super UC to human transfer is unknown. I pray it's abbreviated, but I have no data on which to wager a guess. If a hybrid monster is created from that type of transmittal, the human race has no chance. Think of all of the aforementioned traits minus the death-clock to end their reign of terror."

"Doctor," Mallet began, "we can confirm that your estimated lifespan for the UC, or super UC, is accurate. They're dying off at roughly that threshold. We cannot confirm if any of them were super UC to human transfer. What else can you tell us about them?"

"Keep them on the other side of our border wall. If allowed to run rampant, they will eliminate all life they encounter. Do not, under any circumstances, allow the uninfected to handle the antidote unprotected. If a person so much as gets a drop on their skin, eliminate them. We possess no data on the antidote's half-life, meaning, if the liquid comes in contact with inanimate objects, sterilize them with fire. It's the single element effective in neutralizing the compound."

Mallet fell silent. The answer was obvious, but its implementation could be devastating. Mallet asked McCune to hold and muted the line. "Mister President, I believe the good doctor has given us our path forward."

Train nodded his understanding, then glanced at the speaker.

"Doctor, this is Mallet. Do you possess any data pertaining to the antidote's implementation? Specifically, drift and coverage once it's airborne."

Panic overtook McCune. "Sir, please tell me you're not planning to weaponize the antidote! The only thing we know for certain is that it was successful in creating monsters far more dangerous than the ones currently ravaging our country. We have no means to control it. Releasing it over populated areas will, I repeat, WILL end life on Earth."

Mallet bristled at McCune's sharp tone. "Doctor, does the requested information exist?"

"No sir, it does not. But please give me more time to work on a solution, I'm begging you."

Mallet silently ticked off the tasks to complete prior to moving forward with his quickly developing strategy, the first of which was returning McCune to the lab at Saint Joe's. "Doctor, we'll dispatch an escort to take you back to your laboratory. No matter the outcome of our actions after today, discovering a cure for the virus remains paramount."

"No, thank you, Chairman Mallet. I'm needed here and prefer to stay in this community. Nevertheless, so that I may continue my work, I'm requesting two mobile labs be delivered to me. I'll submit a list of supplies by tomorrow morning. Good day."

The instant the line went quiet, Mallet barked a string of orders, causing the room to explode with activity.

President Train leaned close to Mallet and said, "Chairman, I'm still the Commander-in- Chief. How about you brief me on your strategy."

Acknowledging his overstep, Mallet had Train join him in front of one of the room's large monitors. He brought up a map of Blue States United's West Coast and overlaid it with current wind patterns. "My plan, Mister President, is to disburse the antidote over cities with the largest populations of UC. This should help stop the spread while thinning the ranks of the dead. If we work with the wind patterns, we should be able to cover large swaths of land quickly. I see no value in dispersing the antidote over populated areas of Right America. You have my word; we will keep it as far away from RAM as possible."

Train remained silent for a long moment, the war raging inside of him evident to Mallet. "There must be another way. You're talking about the annihilation of millions... hundreds of millions of people. Can we buy time, focusing on clearing RAM of infected, then weigh our options?"

"Mister President, we've already ceased rescue operations in BSU to focus exclusively on RAM soil. The few remaining pockets of BSU survivors we were in contact with have gone dark."

Mallet turned back to the screen and ordered the display of drone and satellite images of RAM Entry Points. Hundreds of thousands of UCs were assaulting each Entry Point with equal numbers en route to join them.

"Sir, these pictures were taken yesterday. The siege at our gates continues and grows larger by the hour. It is only a matter of time before they overrun our defenses. Our munitions resupply is strained beyond capacity. A Black Hawk crash-landed a mere seventy-five feet from Entry Point Four's gate. We lost the crew, but if it had crashed into the gate, hundreds of thousands of monsters would have poured into RAM."

Mallet took an effectual pause before continuing, "Sir, this is the only option we have to stem the tide, quickly, and conserve resources. And quite frankly, sir, RAM is in no position to fight an army of Blue Savages or super UCs, or whatever you want to call them."

When Train spoke, his voice was heavy with regret. "Move forward. I'll take responsibility for our actions. It's my call." He glanced at the expectant faces surrounding him. "God have mercy on our souls."

McCune slammed the helmet to the tiled floor, fear and rage battling for control. He locked Lucas in a hard stare. "Sergeant, we haven't the resources to fight this enemy if we allow it inside our borders. Enjoy this day. I fear it may be our last."

Pat's panic grew. She had to get out of there. Get to the community's storage area and inventory their supplies. What she'd heard made one thing crystal clear: Supply runs were canceled until this new threat was stopped.

CHAPTER 33 – ANGER

Olaf stood next to Darline, successfully blocking my exit from the room. "I need to get out of here. I need to do something, or I'll lose my mind."

Darline pushed further into the room, forcing me to take a step back. "You should wait until the IV bag is empty."

"It's empty enough," I said while yanking on the needle and instantly regretting it. "Well, maybe I'll leave it in for now. But the second it comes out, I'm leaving."

"Good idea, Otto. You're pretty beat up and lost a fair amount of blood. You need the fluids and antibiotics," Olaf said from behind Darline.

Disregarding the advice, I let my anger take control. "He's going to die, Darline. Willis is going to die. He's trapped in some nameless motel… and he's alone. He's going to die alone. That's not how it should end for him. He's a good man."

Darline moved to console me with an embrace, but I pulled away. "I wished him good luck when he was leaving. It's my fault. I jinxed him, and now he's going to die."

As I began pacing back and forth, the IV line caught on the bed and ripped from my hand, splashing blood over the bed and floor. Olaf pushed past Darline and grabbed some gauze from the medical tray Durrell had left behind. He covered the wound and applied pressure to staunch the bleeding. Olaf secured the gauze with tape and released his grip on my arm.

"Well, seems I've finished the IV; time to go," I said, taking a step towards the door. As I halved the distance to freedom, a gurney appeared in the doorway, trapping me in the room. I prepared a verbal assault for the person responsible for blocking my path when I noticed the gurney's passenger, a fully anesthetized and slack-jawed Lisa.

The gurney bounced and slammed its way through a doorway not built to accommodate its size, followed by Sabrina. Her appearance reminded me of every battlefield nurse I'd seen in the hundreds of war-themed movies I'd watched over the years.

"You need to move, Otto. And you need to get your ass back in bed." She glanced at my bloodied hand and shook her head. "You are a special kind of crazy. Get in bed; I'll reinsert the IV after I get Lisa situated." Her tone left no room for discussion, so I plopped onto the bed like a scolded schoolboy awaiting his dunce cap.

Watching her struggle in the tight confines would have normally been my battlecry to bust chops. But I didn't have it in me; my mind raced as quickly as my pulse, and my heartbeat echoed in my ears. My anger was winning!

Sabrina locked the wheels on Lisa's gurney and pivoted to face me. "Lay down, Otto. We're busy, and I don't have time to play nursemaid." She glanced in Olaf's direction and said, "We're prepping your son for surgery. You should visit him before he's sedated."

Olaf was moving before Sabrina finished speaking.

Attention back to me, she continued. "Lisa needs to be brought out of anesthesia. I'm going back to assist with Aden, Olaf's son's surgery. Think you can handle waking her up?"

Darline chirped in and assured Sabrina *we* would take care of Lisa. Her emphasis on *we* bought her my disapproving glare, which she ignored.

Sabrina attached a fresh IV and warned me not to waste any more of their valuable supplies, then hurried from the room.

Tethered to my IV, and salty, I bumped Lisa's bed with my foot repeatedly until she rustled under the gurney's crisp white sheets.

"Hey, Otto. Why the hell are you in my bedroom?" Lisa said with a dry, scratchy voice as her eyes fluttered open. "Where's my slim yet stunningly handsome man?" A sound similar to sandpaper on hardwood followed as she worked her mouth in circles, searching for moisture. "I'm thirsty. Get me some water. And you didn't answer my question. Why are you in my bedroom? Are you a Peeping Tom? Perv!" Her voice was growing in volume.

"Calm down, Lisa. I'm not in your bedroom; you're in mine. Don't you remember what happened between us last night?" Effectual pause and an evil grin. "The passion that exploded as our bodies became one, the years of sexual tension finally released. It was unlike anything I've ever experienced."

Lisa's eyes bulged but remained unfocused, the anesthesia still clouding her mind.

"It'll be difficult telling Darline and Dillan, but we must. We can't hide from this, and we owe it to them. After we tell them, we'll be together… forever."

"Water, get me some water… NOW!" She would have been screaming if her mouth weren't desert-dry.

From my perch on the edge of my bed, I held out the bottle of water Sabrina had left behind.

Lisa moved her heavily damaged left arm and screeched in agony. "You rotten son-of-a-bitch," she hissed as she switched to her right hand and snatched the bottle from me. Horror washed over her face. "How could you, Otto? Why would you? I hate you! Where's Dillan? I've got to talk to him, explain that this was a mistake, I'll tell him you took advantage of me." She took a long pull from the bottle and swished it around her mouth before swallowing. "He's going to think it's yours," she whined, sounding on the verge of tears as her head swiveled back and forth.

"What's Dillan going to think is mine?"

"Our baby. I'm pregnant, you oaf. Why do you think I stayed home when FST1 went on the supply run? I got suspicious after

I'd had morning sickness a couple of days in a row, and I'm over a month late."

"Um, hey, well, I don't know what to say. Look, I'm kidding about the whole *'We're in love thing.'* You're in the hospital. You were shot, and you're recovering from surgery," I stammered. *Well, I'd gone too far, again.*

Sobering up enough to let her anger take control, Lisa focused as best she could on me. "When I get out of this bed, I will kill you, Otto Hammer. And this time I mean it. I'll kill you in the most gruesome, painful way imaginable."

"Lisa, don't get yourself worked up. You need your rest, and I need to escape this place." My urge to share my thoughts about her reproducing was causing my heavily bandaged and really painful side to throb. This couldn't be happening. A mini-Lisa running around was a terrible image burning into my mind.

"If you utter a word of this to anyone, especially Dillan, I'll pull all of your teeth with my bare hands. Now, where is Dillan!"

"Relax. Darline went to find him after you came out of surgery. He'll be here any second. He doesn't know?"

"No, I snuck a pregnancy test from the community supplies after he left to give FST1 his list. Please, Otto, please don't tell him."

"Tell me what?"

Dillan's voice about scared me out of my skin. Spinning on my bed to face him, I blurted out, "Willis isn't coming back, Dillan. Lisa thought it would upset you; she asked me to keep it to myself. I talked to him about an hour ago. Seems our government unleashed a fresh hell on the world in the form of a failed antidote. He's been exposed to it, and...."

"We'll talk later. Right now, I need some time with Lisa," Dillan interrupted, a mixture of exhaustion and worry washing over his features. "Otto, can you give us a minute?"

"I'd love to, but I'm being held hostage by Nurse Ratchet and this IV," I said while holding the IV tubing up for his viewing pleasure.

He walked between my bed and Lisa's gurney and removed the bag from the nail in the wall on which it had been suspended. "You look healthy enough to walk; there's room in the triage area," he said, smiling and handing me the bag.

"Dillan, your defenses worked, man. You saved this community. This attack was exactly what I feared would happen after seeing Entry Point One. Only I doubted we'd live through one." I paused, allowing dozens of emotions to sort themselves out. "Thank you. We're alive because of you."

Still smiling, Dillan placed his hand on my shoulder and bobbed his head towards the door. "Like I said, Otto, we'll talk later."

I stood to leave and stole a quick glance at Lisa as an unspoken *thank you* flashed across her exhausted features.

CHAPTER 34 – LOCKDOWN

Forty minutes later, Darline and I pushed through the clinic's door. The smell of battle still hung heavy in the air. The first sight to greet me was the gore-smeared International with Randy, Olaf, and Jackson inspecting it through the crust of human remains it had collected while pummeling the dead. It appeared as if Olaf had introduced himself and was already making friends.

Stone was standing ten yards away, staring into the sky. Following his gaze, I quickly found the object holding his attention. A Black Hawk hovered in the distance; my guess would be a quarter-mile to our north.

Jackson was the first to see my battered, slow-moving body. "Look what the cat dragged in," he said as he walked in my direction. "Well, at least you didn't use your head as a weapon this time."

Randy brushed past Jackson and picked up speed on his way to greet me. He held his arms out; it appeared he was planning to hug me. An action my throbbing side promised to protest. "Oh God, Randy, please don't touch me."

The effect my words had on him reminded me of a scolded puppy. His pace slowed as his arms lowered to his sides.

"Hey, chin up, I still love ya. My body just can't take one of your bear hugs."

His smile returned, and he moved in and placed his hands on the sides of my face. He tried to speak, but his words hitched in his throat. He stared at me for a long minute before wiping at his eyes.

Olaf and Jackson had joined us, and each displayed wide smiles. And rightfully so. We had repelled a massive attack, experienced minimal casualties, Olaf's son was getting much needed medical care, and our walls had held.

We could now focus on thriving, on growing our home. I noticed that Stone wasn't sharing in the moment; he hadn't stopped staring at the Hawk, and his expression grew darker by the second.

"Hey, Stone. No words for your wounded brother?" I yelled to him.

Nothing. He didn't even flinch.

Leaning on his weaponized cane, Olaf seemed to put the puzzle together. "Something isn't right. That bird hasn't moved in the last forty minutes. And her gun appears to be hot."

"Air support; it's providing air support for ground operations. I'm with Olaf. Something isn't right. UCs are easy enough to identify and kill on the ground. Should be like shooting fish in a barrel for an airborne Black Hawk. We need to locate Lucas, find out what the hell's happening outside our gate," Stone said.

The mention of Lucas reminded me of Willis; he'd have been our POC in times like these. I realized that the men standing around me didn't know about Willis, and it was my gut-wrenching duty to break the news. My mouth opened as a voice from the clinic reached us. "Olaf, Aden is out of surgery."

Olaf moved towards the clinic, then stopped. "Can't thank you enough for this," he said, his eyes watery. "You all saved my boy."

I nodded and reached out to shake his hand. "I think we're even. I'd have bled out on the floor of an abandoned house if you and Russ hadn't found me."

As if on cue, Olaf's truck rumbled to a stop next to the International. A frazzled-looking towhead emerged from the large Ram pickup. "Someone could have warned me about Pat! We thought Otto was the reason she was so mean. Apparently, she doesn't like anyone! All I was trying to do was deliver the deer meat, and she treated me like an enemy spy. She threatened to smack the plaque off my teeth. Who says that?"

Darline smiled. "You must be Russ. Pat radioed me about you; said you were rude and that she put you in your place."

Olaf ended the exchange by telling the bewildered man to join him in the clinic.

As the two disappeared behind the door of our makeshift hospital, Lucas emerged, her edge less sharp than I was used to. She quickly joined us and yelled for Stone to do the same.

Addressing the semi-circle of battle-worn faces, she didn't mince words. "We have a situation developing just to the north of the community." The group fidgeted nervously, forcing her to pause. When the anxiety seemed to die down, she continued, "You have no doubt noticed the Black Hawk and are probably wondering why it's still on scene."

She hit each of us with a hard stare, then continued. "Two CDC operatives have gone missing. We found one with a broken neck and a missing throat inside their Humvee. Our Bradley also encountered, and eliminated, a group of UCs that had separated from the main herd. They displayed tactical awareness. They sought cover, attempted to avoid our BFV, and moved as a singular unit."

"What are you getting at, Sergeant?" Stone asked.

A sinking feeling took hold. I knew where Lucas was going, so I interjected, "Look, guys. I have some bad news. And it may tie into this." I pulled a deep calming breath and plowed forward before I lost my nerve and my composure. "Willis isn't coming home. He's been infected by, or exposed to, an antidote meant to counteract the virus. Unfortunately, its side-effects are proving far worse than the virus itself."

Emotion crept into my voice, so I paused, trying to regain control. The disbelieving stares matched mine. Willis, our friend, was gone.

Lucas broke our reverie. "Camp Hopkins is working on the chain of events that led to their Humvee being abandoned. All we know is they were after Doctor McCune.

"McCune plans on talking to Sergeant Timmons as well. He's trying to determine what happened after he escaped. Some of what we witnessed today may simply be evolution, but the scene in the Humvee doesn't fit that scenario. My gut tells me that something escaped from Saint Joe's and found its way into that Humvee and brought the antidote's side-effects with it."

Stone's eyes nearly exploded from their sockets. He held up a hand, cutting Lucas off. His radio was at his mouth an instant later. "Will, this is Stone. Get everyone inside the gate and lock it down. No time to explain, just do it."

"On it," Will answered without question.

Lucas, red-faced that a civilian had recognized the potential threat before she did, barked the same order to her team but told someone named Zahra to keep her BFV onsite.

I glanced at Lucas and asked, "Can you keep that Bradley here, at least until we determine what's happening?"

Shaking her head before I finished, Lucas answered, "Hopkins plans on sending more troops to help search for the missing operator. So no, RAM won't grant Otto Hammer the personal use of a Bradley in the foreseeable future. Actually, ever."

I stiffened, catching Darline's attention in the process. She knew what was about to happen if I stayed. "Okay, that's enough. Otto needs his rest. We're going home, and I *forbid* you boys from visiting him," she said as we moved towards the street.

"Babe, I can't walk home from here. Make Sergeant Lucas drive us home," I said, eager to continue our conversation regarding the Bradley.

"No, Otto, Sergeant Lucas cannot drive us home. Jackson, we need a ride, NOW."

CHAPTER 35 – HIDE

Two hours later, I found myself watching the community put itself back together from my living room window. It was a frustrating experience. I wanted to take part in the effort of rebuilding our community. It also gave me too much time to think.

I sat on our couch, sidelined once again and missing my younger man's body and the promises it had once held: indestructibility and eternal youth. I turned away from the window, grabbed another Ibuprofen, and swallowed it sans water.

With Darline outside helping the community, our home was eerily quiet. I stretched out on the couch and stared at the ceiling, smiling when I found the sections I had missed when we painted it. I had been promising Darline I'd repaint them for almost ten years now. "Nope, I'd rather fight zombies than paint the ceiling," I said through a soft chuckle.

The memories of better times raced around my head, killing any hope of catching some shuteye. *How did we end up here? Does life have any meaning beyond living through the next loss of a friend, the next attack on our home? Will I be next?* I shook the thoughts away and slid my hand down my face.

Darline poked her head through the front door a few restless minutes later. "Hey, are you sleeping?" she asked through a beaming smile.

I raised my hand above the back of the couch and waved. "I'm up, and I have a question for you. It's about life."

"No time, you have visitors."

"Hey, you said no visitors. And I agree. Also, I'm not in the mood. Unless they can answer my question about life," I whined.

"Hey Otto, you sound like a little girl." It was *Lucas*, and she was leading FST1, along with Lewis, Stevenson, and Jackson, into my house.

"Sergeant, I can't thank you enough for what you did for us today. Without you and your team, I'd probably be bleeding to death waiting for the community to quell the attack. But I'm in no mood for your red-eyed nastiness."

"Quell, that's a fancy word for such a small brain," Lucas retorted.

Darline had already heard enough. "Okay, knock it off. I have to get back to work. Can I trust you two not to kill each other? You know what, I don't care. Randy, Stone, these two are your problem. If they break anything, I'm holding you responsible."

After Darline slammed the door and her muffled tirade faded, Lucas looked at me and said, "She's a mean one; doesn't even care if I kill her husband."

"Right? I'm surrounded by mean people that don't appreciate the stress that comes with being me."

I answered her questioning stare. "I'm always running headlong into the fray, with no regard for personal safety, to save my loved ones."

"Holy sh… You don't believe that, do you? Don't answer; I already know."

The group ignored my ramblings and took positions around the living room. The grim looks on their faces told me I should shut up and listen.

"I received some INTEL," Lucas started. "Our search team believes they spotted the missing CDC operative. They spotted the target running for cover to avoid the team."

The news made me attempt to sit up, and I quickly regretted it. Instead, I grabbed a couch cushion and propped my head up, giving me a better view of Lucas.

"Why would he avoid being found? No rational person would purposely get caught alone, outside our gates." My eyes went wide when understanding found me.

"Looks like you just figured it out, Otto. And to remove all doubt, the description of the target matches what Doctor McCune observed during the antidotes human trials." Lucas glanced around the room. "McCune spoke with Sergeant Timmons from Saint Joe's. He confirmed that the CDC goons engaged a level two UC being tested for its response to the antidote. It appears we have a hybrid monster resulting from that level two UC to human transfer."

"So we *do* have a 'Twenty Eight Days Later' situation on our hands?"

"Not following. What's that mean?" Lucas asked.

"It's a movie that scared Otto out of his skin. In short, it means fast, very aggressive, intelligent zombies," Randy said.

"Got it, and yes. We have that Twenty whatever scenario playing out as we speak," Lucas began, "only this time, you're being asked to write the happy ending."

"You never saw the movie, did you? It's not the best ending. The sequel is even worse. No, we're in trouble." I paused, glancing at each member of FST1. "We need to get ready for the fight of our lives."

Lucas leaned forward in her seat, concern dominating her features. "Otto, there's more. The Joint Chiefs are pulling ninety percent of ground forces to the entry points and strategic locations along the border wall. Mallet is planning an offensive on BSU soil. He's concerned it'll cause a surge of UCs to hit RAM. He's deploying us to fortify the troops already guarding our border."

"Well, aren't you a ray of bright sunshine?" I began while repositioning myself on the couch. "Seeing we're going to be on our own, fighting a new and deadly UC monster, how about you reconsider leaving us that Bradley?"

"Still a negative on the BFV, Otto. But I'll make sure we resupply the community with ammo and medical supplies." Lucas stood and nodded. "You'll hear from me within twenty-four hours on the resupply."

With that, Lewis and Stevenson followed her through the door.

I counted the faces in the room and realized one was missing. "Where's Andy?"

"I'm down here!" Andy's voice sprang from the basement, nearly jolting me from the couch.

"Andy, why are you sneaking around my basement? How long have you been there? You scared the crap outta me."

As Andy emerged from hiding, he filled me in on the circumstances that led him to my home. "Long enough to know that you should repaint your ceiling. And I really don't understand why I'm hiding. Darline snatched me from guarding the gate and dragged me here. Said she didn't have time to explain. When she brought you home, I figured she'd tell you; when she didn't, I figured she was hiding me from you. I'm really confused, Otto." Andy stood at the end of the couch, staring at the ceiling.

"You're right. It should be repainted," he said, then added, "you talk to yourself, a lot."

The entirety of FST1 was staring at my ceiling when a hard knock shook the front door, followed by Pat bursting through it. She followed the group's gaze and said, "You should repaint your ceiling."

"Thanks for offering. I'll get you a roller and drop cloth after the apocalypse ends. Right now, though, I'd like to know why you're in my house."

My question grabbed everyone's attention, and all eyes fell on Pat in anticipation of her smacking me down. Instead, she focused on Andy. "Thank God. I hadn't been able to find you. I was worried some government goons had already snatched you."

Andy's confusion grew deeper and he asked, "What's going on, Pat? Why would *government goons* want to snatch me? I'm getting a bit freaked out. Can someone please tell what the hell's going on?"

His expectant gaze floated to each person in the room, then locked on Pat.

"Take a seat, Andy. I have some information."

Pat went through the conversation she'd overheard between McCune and an unknown person or persons. It tied into what Lucas had told us about the UC variant possibly running loose in the streets outside our barriers. Then she cleared up the confusion surrounding Andy hiding in my basement.

"You will not be a guinea pig, Andy. Not on my watch." Her tone removed all doubt that she meant what she said.

"Nor do I want to be a guinea pig, Pat. But if they're only looking for blood samples, maybe some small tissue samples, I'm okay with it. It's a small price to pay if it helps them find a cure."

"We've already supplied them with blood samples, a lot of them. What do you think they want now, a sample of your brain, heart, maybe your intestines?"

Andy appeared to deflate into the cushions of his chair. "I'm not okay with that, but if I hold the key to saving my family, your family, or every person on the planet, I think I owe it to humanity to at least see what they want from me."

Pat waved him off. "Nope, not today, not ever. These idiots have accomplished nothing outside of making things worse. They get blood, and that's it."

Changing the subject, she shifted to the new threat lurking on the horizon. "I'm canceling all scavenging runs until we have a handle on what this *hybrid* monster is capable of. And I'm *ordering* this team to develop a plan to eliminate the threat. Work with your military *friends* and figure something out."

Will spoke up. "Pat, Sergeant Lucas informed us we're on our own; no military assistance. For the next couple of weeks, anyway." He paused, searching for the words that wouldn't send Pat into full-tilt crazy. "We need those supply runs, Pat. Winter is around the corner. The late start hampered our food production. Our MRE stash will probably get us through, if, and only if we start strict rationing immediately. We only picked up a few of the propane conversion kits. Not to mention we need to locate and secure sufficient amounts of propane. We can't stop the supply runs; we simply can't."

Holding Will in a withering stare, Pat appeared to be digesting the reality behind his words. "Well then, what's your plan?"

"We don't have one yet. But we will soon enough."

"Then this is how it'll work. The gates remain locked until you have one, and execute it." She shifted abruptly to address Andy, causing him to flinch. "As for you, your name is now Ralph. And it will remain Ralph until we determine if we can trust the doctor. He's having portable labs delivered to our little slice of heaven, so apparently, he's planning on setting up shop behind our walls. That should tell you how much he trusts our government. It also means you are to steer clear of him and those labs. I'll get the word out that we're now calling you Ralph. I'll work with McCune on supplying him with blood samples. If the good doctor requests anything else, I will deny his request. Have I been clear?" She held the group in her fiery eyes until we confirmed our understanding. Sweet baby Jesus, that woman is intimidating.

She stood to leave, then froze. "One more thing. The next time any of you sends someone to the supply area, tell me ahead of time. I nearly beat a man senseless today before I figured out who he was and that he was delivering our venison. Pay attention, people, we're in a war." She stomped through the front door, slamming it behind her.

Stone finally broke our stunned silence. "Anyone want to tell her we had nothing to do with Russ dropping off the meat?"

"Sure," Andy started, "right after I tell her I don't care for my new name."

Their comments brought some welcome but short-lived laughter.

No time for levity. We needed a plan.

CHAPTER 36 – STENCH

It was a week after the attack on our community, and the heavy equipment Lucas had requested was nowhere in sight. The stench from the rotting bodies littering the ground around our community had reached unbearable levels.

The putrid bodies created a second potentially deadly situation. An immeasurable amount of pests had descended on our community. It started as a wall of flies so thick it was impossible to see the bodies beneath them. Carrion birds soon followed in numbers large enough to blot out the sun. When they were startled into flight, the effect often plunged us into mid-day darkness, not to mention their foul droppings were becoming a serious health hazard. The birds unable to fight through the masses to get to the putrid feast found our remaining, un-harvested crops easy pickings.

However, the reason for our meeting under the northeast tower was the arrival of hundreds of rats. Sometimes they'd cluster together in numbers so large sections of the ground appeared to be an undulating living organism. The lack of human intervention had allowed their population to grow unchecked for months, and we'd unknowingly rung the dinner bell.

Our efforts to keep them from breaching our barrier proved futile and led to several members being bitten. They found their way into our homes and our community storage area, threatening our emergency food supply. Our community was turning into an unlivable cesspool.

"We launch our plan, and we launch it today. First order of business is to clean this nightmare up!" I barked while taking in the fear-invoking image outside our wall.

In a compromise with Pat, our original plan called for two days of observing the area for signs of the missing CDC operative turned hybrid UC. But before we knew it, the current plague had taken hold, forcing us to divert resources to fighting the invasion of pests currently overwhelming us.

I turned to face the others as they stared at the horrific scene from our perch on the earthen section of the northeast barrier. I had donned a raincoat to protect against the bird droppings that often rained from the sky without warning, coupled with ankle-high boots to guard against rat bites. My outfit drew accusations of overreaction from the team, but thanks to Alfred Hitchcock, I'm not a fan of birds or the fact that they use the world as their toilet.

"How, Otto? How do we clean them up?" Pat asked while gesturing to the gruesome landscape.

"We find more dump trucks, like the Internationals, and fit them with snowplows. That should allow us to push the dead away from the wall and into piles. Then we locate backhoes and use them to load the bodies into the trucks, move the carcasses as far away as possible, then burn them. They won't fit into our burn pits. We can dump them in the mall parking lot and burn them there. It should lower the risk of the fire spreading to a minimum and keep this plague to our south."

"Where do we find the equipment?" Stone asked, not moving his gaze from the dystopian landscape.

"The city's service garage should have everything we need. At least they did the last time I drove by the garage on my way to work. Front-end loaders would be more efficient. They have larger payloads than backhoes and should fill the dump trucks twice as fast." Tesha nailed it. Speed was imperative. The teams operating the heavy equipment would pose easy targets for both the pests and UCs. We needed to operate in double-time if we wanted the plan to work.

"Jackson, are both Internationals ready to go?"

"I finished up-armoring the second one yesterday, Otto."

"Okay then, we roll in twenty," I said as a giant bird-shit hit the edge of my raincoat's hood, speckling my face in nastiness. "Son of a BITCH! It's like they heard us talking about them. Make it twenty-five. I need to scour this off with boiling water before I do anything else."

Thankfully, their hysterical laughter made it impossible to talk, sparing me from their childish ridicule.

I stormed home with a slight limp caused by my attempt to protect my sutured wound. It was healing nicely but remained extremely sensitive. I hadn't taken a single practice shot or participated in any training since being stabbed. FST1 started using the rats for target practice but stopped because of our dwindling ammunition supply. Not only hadn't the heavy equipment arrived, but Lucas had also never delivered the promised resupply of ammunition. In fact, the only pledge the government had delivered on was the mobile labs and medical supplies McCune had insisted we receive.

The stench, bird crap, and occasional rat scurrying across my path during my trudge home combined to infuriate me! I entered through our sunroom and stripped to my skivvies, then tossed my clothes into a trash bag set up for just such an occasion.

"This is such bullshit!" I bellowed upon entering the kitchen and flipping the faucet to hot. While I waited for the water to reach optimal sanitizing temperature, I realized Darline hadn't responded.

I turned to call out for her and found her note on the counter. She had gone to rat-proof the community storage area. The note set me off. We've lived through a zombie flipping apocalypse, and now a bunch of rodents were threatening to take us out.

Turning back to the faucet, I found steam billowing from the sink. In a controlled rage, I stuck my face into the scalding stream.

Funny how skin melting from a person's skull can cause them to lose track of their surroundings. I confirmed this to be true because it happened when my skin sent the message to my brain that I was an idiot. I jerked my head to the side, smashing it off the inside of the sink, causing it to bounce back into the lava flow pouring from the faucet. Again my head jerked and slammed against the inside of the sink. I had become a human pinball.

I broke the cycle when I regained control and pulled my head up and shut off the water. My face felt raw, my head throbbed, but I was no longer covered in bird poop.

CHAPTER 37 – GLIMPSE

I crawled carefully into the cab of the International 4300 being piloted by Jackson. With Jay occupying the space between us, the cramped cab was uncomfortable as I shifted around, attempting to protect my side from being jolted by Jay's elbow.

"Jay, who conned you into joining us?"

"Your brother. Told me something about picking up a front-end loader and needing me to drive it back. You better pray it has a closed cab. If we find one, that is."

As we waited for the Hummer and the other International to pull through the gate, I caught Jackson staring at me from the corner of my eye.

"What's on your mind, *Jackson?*"

"Your face is awfully red and shiny. Looks painful, too."

"I'm in no mood, Jackson."

"Is that a blister on your cheek?" He was grinning and crawling onto my last nerve.

"Seriously, I'm in no mood. Just drive the damn truck and try not to kill us. You're making Jay uncomfortable, so cut the crap."

"Nope, I'm not uncomfortable at all. But I am curious about your face. It looks really uncomfortable."

Thankfully, Tesha's voice crackled over our radio, drawing attention away from my face and back to the mission ahead.

"Listen up, ladies. We stay tight this time. If we run into another herd of UCs, the size of the one that attacked us, we'll be forced to abandon the Hummer. If that happens, pull your rigs up to block our sides, and we'll exit through the windows and into your rigs. Are we clear?"

Both rigs confirmed their understanding and established which side of the Hummer each would cover in case of a forced evacuation.

We'd settled in for the short drive to the city service garage when I noticed something. We hadn't encountered a single UC. RAM's military had done an excellent job of defending our borders, and our city had a relatively small population of UCs; sightings by our tower guards had declined steadily. Nevertheless, we always found at least one of the nasty beasts wandering the streets. So their absence was alarming.

"Jay, Jackson, where did all the zombies disappear to?"

Jay spoke first. "Probably killed most of them during the attack. Don't you think?"

"I'd like to agree with you, Jay. But to Otto's point, Willis and his team found empty shipping containers near the insurgent's headquarters. And I'm sure there were dozens more stashed throughout the city. So those UCs are accounted for. We were still seeing them shambling around just before the attack. Meaning the BSU insurgent hadn't corralled them all. Something isn't right." Jackson glanced in my direction and nodded at the radio.

Taking his cue, I grabbed the radio and hailed the other vehicles to inform them of our observation; both agreed and confirmed they'd noticed the same.

Nerves on edge, I figured talking about Lisa's news might lighten the mood. "So, Lisa, Dillan, and baby make three. I'm happy for them. Although I'm not thrilled at the prospect of having Lisa's spawn running wild in our streets. Seriously, what was Dillan thinking?"

Their bugged eyes and sharp breaths telegraphed that Lisa's *condition* was news to them. "Oh, God, please don't tell anyone, especially Lisa. I figured everyone already knew. Didn't Dillan tell everyone?"

Jackson finally pulled his focus back to the road but was obviously still in shock. "Dillan has been spending all of his time with Lisa. He took her home yesterday, maybe the day before. And considering our current state of affairs, I haven't had time for a social visit. Who told you?"

Angling to move their focus to another subject, I shifted gears to the government's plan to exterminate the UC plague. "Do you think Operation Blue Savage will be successful? I'm guessing it'll make things worse."

My ploy seemed to work; the cab went silent, then I opened my fat mouth. "We should work with Dillan on adding some height to the barrier. If these new UC monsters prove as dangerous as Lucas and McCune led us to believe, we'll need the added security. We should probably install those perimeter alarms, too."

"So, Dillan and Lisa as mom and dad. Are they getting married? Hey, you should perform the ceremony, Otto. That'd be something to see." Jackson's a jerk.

"Come on, Jackson, let it go. And don't tell anyone, including Natalia. Lisa will tell everyone when she's ready. And I can't have her in my house, commiserating with Darline and plotting revenge on me for talking."

I grabbed the radio, attempting to both redirect the conversation and confirm my suspicions. I got Pat on the line and, after several minutes of back and forth, confirmed that the guard towers and foot patrols hadn't observed any UCs for several days.

"This isn't good, guys. Is another insurgent attempting to gather thousands of UCs together to attack us?"

"We don't have the resources to fend off another attack," Jay interjected.

"I know. Ammo production has ground to a virtual halt because of a lack of projectiles. Al's been pulling lead, balancing weights from car rims to cast them old-school-style. Add to that, his team is splitting their time between manufacturing and pest control," I said while staring out the passenger side window, my imagination running wild with images of our home being overrun.

"Not to mention we lost three good people during the attack plus an additional dozen wounded and out of commission."

The cab went silent after Jackson finished. We couldn't do it; not a chance we'd repel another attack even half the size of the last one. I realized we needed the heavy equipment for more than disposing of the bodies. We needed them to help us fight back.

Still staring out the window and trying to control the panic taking root, I caught a flash of brightly colored fabric as we sped past the high school football field. I thought it was simply remnants of clothing stuck in the fence surrounding the stadium, maybe some trash, until it dashed to the left and disappeared from sight.

"Whoa, what the hell was that?" I shouted.

The truck slowed as if responding to my statement. Answering my questioning stare, Jackson confirmed he'd seen it too.

Jay's head swiveled side to side as he tried to figure out what we were talking about. I radioed Tesha. She had seen nothing. Stone confirmed that no one in his truck had seen it either. We decided FST1 would recon the school after securing the equipment and escorting it home.

I was hyper-vigilant as we rumbled up to the service yard gate. The area appeared untouched and empty. But letting our guard down wasn't an option. And I couldn't shake the sensation that something wasn't right.

"Okay, ladies," Tesha started, "looks like they're going to make us work for it. I'm guessing they stored the heavy equipment either in the service garage or the parking lot behind it. Andy will cut the lock; Stone, your team follows me, and we'll search the garage. Jackson, your team will search behind the building. Radio your findings."

"Why does she keep calling us ladies?" I asked.

Ignoring my indignation, Jackson glanced at Jay and asked, "How long will it take to get the plows attached to the trucks?"

Jay appeared to do some quick math before answering. "Good question; depends on the type of hitch and its condition. Regardless, plan on an hour."

Jackson pressed the radio's talk button. "Andy, leave enough padlock to hold the chain in place after we enter. I want to avoid another situation like we ran into at Jay's construction yard."

"Jackson, I'm going to guard the gate. I have a bad feeling, plus we probably stirred up every UC within a mile of here. I'll post up behind that stack of pallets next to the gate," I said while gripping the door handle and preparing to exit the cab.

When our truck entered the yard, I hopped out and bolted for the pallets. "Andy, let Tesha know this *lady* has our six."

He smiled and nodded his understanding as he ran back to the Hummer.

I slapped at my tactical vest, searching for my binoculars. The football field was a straight shot from where I was standing, but it was partially blocked by some pine trees and shrubs. I figured I'd be able to get a decent viewing angle from my position.

After several searches, I finally located my binoculars and started glassing the football field for signs of a UC infestation. I focused on the area where I had spotted the movement just moments ago. Nothing!

"Come on, you nasty prick, where are you?" I whispered and began scanning to the left. There! It happened again—a flash of color, the same bright yellow as before. It looked like a hi-visibility vest, like the type a road or construction crew wears. And it was wrapped around the body of a heavily decayed UC.

I adjusted my focus on the vest-wearing UC, and my breath hitched. It was being dragged behind pine trees skirting the football field's fence. I focused on the beast pulling the yellow-vest-clad UC as it quickly disappeared from sight, but I saw enough to know who it was.

Black ACUs covered mottled, translucent skin. It was the missing CDC operator. I had found the hybrid UC.

CHAPTER 38 – OPERATION BLUE SAVAGE

The surge started three days after RAM dispersed the antidote over selected areas of Blue States United. The initial wave was comprised of regular UCs, the enemy they knew. But something became clear several hours into Operation Savage Blue. An unseen force was smashing the UCs against the wall from behind.

With air support grounded to avoid the accidental spread of the antidote, they were blind to the cause and performed their duty as ordered, cutting down thousands of monsters. Bodies began piling up at the base of the wall. The first layer of dead was quickly covered by a second layer, then a third.

Lucas noticed the mounting bodies and realized the threat. She ordered her team to cease fire and radioed a situation report to Fort Stateline's TOC. Moments later, the entire mile-long barrage abruptly ended, and two drones were soon scouting behind enemy lines.

Mallet had deployed Lucas' team to Entry Point Ten on the Idaho and Washington State border; they were positioned on I-90 in Stateline Village, Idaho, one hundred yards from the entry gate. They were hot, sweaty, and trying to fight a battle wearing MOPP gear designed to protect them from the deadly antidote.

Their location dictated the MOPP gear. Entry Point Ten had been inundated by refugees at the onset of the virus. Now, the area beyond the gate held only countless shambling dead. But the primary concern was Spokane, Washington's location a mere nineteen miles away. When they dispersed the antidote over Spokane, it marked the nearest city to RAM's border to be targeted and posed the greatest threat for antidote drift.

Lucas and thousands of other troops had sheltered in one of two enormous, big-box stores, converted to Entry Point Ten's operations center, until the area was deemed safe for humans to enter.

Seventy-two hours later, Lucas' unit found themselves reengaging the enemy. But this time, they held a significant advantage: a squadron of AH-64 Apache Attack Helicopters hovered to their north and south, cutting down the threat at the rear of the horde being pressed against their gate. The Apaches engaged the battlefield at high altitude and from Right America's side of the wall to minimize rotor-wash pushing the antidote onto RAM's forces.

When the warbird's M230 chain guns rattled to life, Sergeant Lucas gave the command to fire at will. Hundreds of battle rifles answered her order by sending a wall of copper-jacketed death into the advancing monsters. She marched back and forth along the line of soldiers, screaming her encouragement. But she was hiding behind the bravado of her words. In truth, what they were witnessing terrified her.

The drone footage showed tens of thousands of Blue Savages moving into position behind the monsters already clustering at the gate. They moved as an organized fighting unit, exploiting the cover provided by their UC brethren to advance towards the gate unseen.

But the thing that terrified Lucas was when Blue Savages started using UCs as shields against RAM's military barrage. They forced them forward, smashing them against the wall and into the maelstrom, moving from UC to UC to avoid becoming a target.

Lucas recognized that this new threat couldn't be allowed to enter Right America, no matter the cost.

She was lost in the images of her country being overrun until a voice snapped her back to reality. "Sergeant Lucas!" The soldier's name tape identified him as Smith; his face identified him as barely seventeen years old. "These things are acting like the zombies from World War Z."

Lucas followed Smith's outstretched hand to find he was pointing towards the growing pile of twice-dead bodies.

Missing his meaning, Lucas hard-stepped at Smith and barked, "Thank you for sharing your worthless observation, Smith. Now, aim your gun at the monsters and pull the trigger."

Lucas pivoted and took a step just as the firing line fell silent. Her eyes shifted to the AH-64s and found they, too, had ceased fire. She followed the gaze of men and women under her command and pulled a sharp breath. Nothing moved. The onslaught had ended.

"Stateline TOC, this is Sergeant Lucas. I need a SITREP, over."

"Dark Sky Actual for Lucas," the AH-64 squad leader cut in. "This is your SITREP. The Blue Savages are tumbling like dominos. It appears our INTEL was accurate. They're dying en masse. Dark Sky Actual, out."

Train sat quietly watching the drone footage displayed on the war room's half-dozen monitors. Each showed the same scenario playing out across Right America's westernmost states. The antidote had achieved its desired effect: devastation.

The Joint Chiefs stood gathered around one monitor in particular, and Train could swear that none of them had taken a breath in over an hour. Their focus was Stateline, Idaho, and the mounting body count pressing against the wall.

Mallet landed hard in his chair and turned his gaze to Train. "It held, the wall held. But we need to devise a strategy to minimize the stress placed on it, especially when engaging densely populated areas near our border." Mallet stopped and met the stares of his staff. "Mister President, we're also working on a strategy to eliminate the threat on RAM soil."

Train nodded solemnly, noticing that Mallet appeared to have aged twenty years over the last seventy-two hours. "Chairman, get to work on that strategy. It's time to take our country back."

CHAPTER 39 – OPERATION MICRO BLUE

A week after the successful execution of Operation Blue Savage, Lucas found herself swiping at her eyes, but the stinging liquid continued to pour into them from overhead. She ordered her troops to use their camelbacks to flush the blue liquid from their faces. Lucas knew it was hopeless but refused to die without a fight.

She stormed down the firing line, helping soldiers clear the sticky liquid from their skin. Her anger unchecked, she lowered her boom-mic and screamed, "What the hell just happened? I've got two hundred soldiers covered in blue liquid. Someone confirm: Is this the antidote?"

Lucas noticed a pitch change from the AH-64's turbine. "I say again, was my team exposed to the antidote?" With an eye on the squadron of attack helicopters, she watched in horror as they moved into formation to the rear of her team's position. Lucas recognized it for what it was: attack formation.

"Hostiles, twelve-o'clock, Sergeant."

Lucas twisted around to face Lewis. Covered in gummy liquid, the soldier's battle rifle was tracking hundreds of targets shambling towards the gate. She stole another look at the gunships, their 30mm chain guns lowered in her direction. She understood what it meant. Lucas gave a sharp salute to the pilots, turned her back to them, and gave the order for her team to open fire on the monsters.

***

Sergeant Major McMaster slammed the After Action Report to his desk, causing Nathan to flinch. The action was out of character for his father; the elder McMaster was an emotional rock. He'd never seen the man lose his temper or act out of frustration.

"We lost Lucas and her squad today," his father growled.

The news stunned Nathan. Sergeant Lucas was an exemplary leader. Her team was comprised of battle-hardened, well-trained, and fearless warriors. True tip of the spear soldiers.

"What the hell happened?"

The sergeant major nodded at the AAR. "Read it. The short version is the JCS was overconfident, began Operation Micro Blue too soon, and it cost hundreds of soldiers their lives."

Nathan pulled the report from the desk. After two minutes, he realized the magnitude of the challenges that had caused the launch of Operation Micro Blue to fail spectacularly.

Mallet had designed the operation to ease the burden placed on the gates and wall at the entry points without using the C130 air disbursement, as they had during Operation Blue Savage, close to RAM's borders. Although well-intentioned, a government desperate to slow the virus' spread and defend its borders had rushed it into action.

The teams had set up behind steel barriers strategically placed two hundred yards from Entry Point One. They'd launched M252 mortars packed with the antidote into the UCs massing at the gate. Using mortars loaded with minimal explosive charges as the delivery system reduced their horizontal blast radius, lowering the possibility of airborne drift and decreasing the possibility of the new variant infecting the frontline soldiers.

Attack copters patrolled outside the defensive perimeter, as they had in Stateline, Idaho, while infantry troops held ground positions.

The operation went sideways after the first 81mm mortar struck a tanker truck filled with gasoline which had been mired in the gridlock outside Entry Point One. The resulting explosion sent the antidote in every direction, and the subsequent mortar blasts supplied additional antidote to the drift. The military had ignored the forecast for twenty-mile-an-hour winds, which pushed the antidote to the defensive positions and saturated the unprotected troops on the ground.

The AH-64s were forced to fire on their own infected RAM ground troops.

Nathan's head snapped up to meet his father's eyes. "Why weren't they wearing MOPP gear?"

"We ran out of them. They burned the ones used during Operation Blue Savage after the teams disengaged from our wall out west. JCS claims they acted out of an abundance of caution to avoid accidental contamination. That action decimated our MOPP gear supply. They knew of the situation but moved forward anyway."

McMaster ran a hand down his face. "You don't have to read anymore; it doesn't get better. But we're taking a walk."

In silence, the men rounded the corner from Trooper Drive to Kitty Drive, heading towards the PX building.

Nathan noticed the sergeant major surveying the area, for what he didn't know. "Dad, what's with the cloak and dagger routine?"

The elder McMaster responded without slowing his stride. "The rest of the AAR talked about the military's intent to move more refugees to Riley and moving us to ad hoc Forward Operating Bases. Then increase the pace of Operation Micro Blue. Even after the cluster at Entry Point One, the JCS still sees value in OMB and plans to move forward."

"When are they planning on moving us?"

"Two weeks from today. They're activating Fort Riley for the mission. Son, I can't stop them from sending you into that cluster... if we're still here."

Nathan slammed to a stop, faced his father, and locked him with an angry glare. "Dad, are you suggesting I go AWOL? That I shirk my responsibilities?"

"Nothing of the sort, Nathan, but understand this. Our family has dedicated its entire life to this country. We have both run headlong into the fire. Hell, I nearly lost you to government bureaucracy. We've sacrificed enough. I will not allow them to send you to your death, a horrible death, on a whim. I can't stop them from unleashing this new variant on our country, but I sure as hell can stop them from making you one of its victims."

"Well, I'm not deserting, so what's your plan?"

"I submitted our transfer paperwork this morning. Camp Hopkins is now low on troops and people to lead them. They're tasked with a renewed search and rescue operation and need soldiers like you. Our country needs soldiers like you. We can house at that community Willis moved his family to."

The mention of Willis jolted Nathan. "Any update on him?"

"Nothing since his last transmission. He sounded animalistic towards the end of our conversation. I'm not sure what was happening to him, but I know he's not coming home. We've scrubbed the mission, permanently."

The revelation brought understanding to Nathan. He now knew why his father was moving them.

"Alright, let's pack up. But you need to understand, I'm still a soldier, and I refuse to cower from this fight."

Sergeant Major McMaster smiled at his warrior son and nodded. "You'll be fighting, son, fighting the enemy you can see."

CHAPTER 40 – BOXERS

From our perch in an open window of what appeared to be a high school science room, overlooking the football field, Randy stared at me through his patented crazy eyes.

"Why the crazy eyes, Randy?"

"Did you hear the words that just came out of your mouth, Otto?" Randy asked, nearly breaking to full voice from his stage whisper.

"I did, Randy. And before you ask, I actually picked my words carefully. I didn't want to overwork that tiny brain of yours."

Randy's right eye twitched, more like spasmed. He pulled a deep breath and spoke through clenched teeth. "You couldn't have understood the words coming out of that hole in your face, Otto. Let me repeat them to you."

"I'm good, Randy," I interrupted while waving a dismissive hand in his face. "And I still think it's possible. We could start thinning the herd while we wait for FST1 to return. We own the element of surprise, a tactically superior position, and enough ammo to end this now."

Randy shook his head, returning his gaze to the football field where over a hundred monsters shambled aimlessly around the once immaculately cared-for monument to wasted taxpayer money.

I glanced around the classroom, once again cursing the voters who had approved the tax levy that built this school. I realized that this was the first time I had stepped foot inside its walls, even though my tax dollars paid for it. "Man, if I had that money back, we'd have a lot more ammo."

Again, Randy locked me in his crazy stare.

"Randy, just keep looking for the zombie wearing the bright yellow vest. The hybrid seems fixated on him. We'll wait for the others to return and follow the original plan. However, I still think my plan is better."

The original plan was simple. Randy and I had stayed behind to recon the area and monitor the CDC operative turned hybrid UC's movements. After the frontend loader and dump trucks were delivered to the community, one of the newly acquired plow trucks would return along with one of our up-armored International 4300s.

A quarter-mile from the field, Stone and Andy would dismount and take positions on rooftops of low-slung outbuildings located to the northeast and northwest of the field. The plow truck would then block the main gate while the up-armored truck blocked the smaller emergency exit. Once in place, Andy and Stone would open up with M249s while Randy and I focused on killing the infected CDC agent. The crossfire we were planning would tear the rotting corpses to pieces, with no risk of friendly fire killing our team. Only problem was, we couldn't locate the hybrid.

The number of monsters visible inside the field's confines was much smaller than expected, but as Randy watched through his binoculars, it became clear that smaller numbers didn't equate to less dangerous.

He slapped my arm, bringing my focus back to the field. "Look at that! He's bringing more monsters to the field."

I glassed the area he was pointing to, and what I saw nearly stopped my heart. The black-ACU-clad hybrid UC was using a push-broom to herd three terribly decayed UCs through the main gate. Once through the gate, he closed and secured it behind him, locking them inside.

It moved with purpose to the center of the mass as it waved its arms wildly above its head. The setting conjured up images of a football coach admonishing his team after a sloppy practice. Whatever this new variant was, it had to be stopped.

Randy brought his rifle's scope to his eye and panned back and forth until he landed on the hybrid. "Otto," he started with fear creeping into his voice, "it looks like it's yelling at them, or trying to."

Randy's scope was much more powerful than my small binoculars, affording him a higher level of detail. But I trusted him and said, "Take the shot, Randy. We can deal with the other UCs afterwards."

He pulled his AR in tight as his finger moved to the trigger. His breathing slowed, then stopped. His finger began taking up the pre-travel. Recognizing the sequence, I went silent, knowing Randy was in the zone. This monster was going to die in three, two... static filled the air, causing Randy to flinch, sending his shot down and right, clipping his target in the shoulder and spinning it to the ground.

I launched a string of obscenities as Randy scrambled to reacquire his target. I watched through my binoculars as the wounded monster grabbed another beast and used it as a shield while zigzagging to the exit.

"Randy, this one's trouble. We have to stop it. Do you have another shot?"

"Not a kill shot. But I'm going to try to slow it down. Feel free to join in, Otto. More bullets are always better!"

"I say again, Stone for Otto or Randy, we're moving into position."

Ruger tight to my shoulder, I paused to respond to Stone's second broadcast. "Get your asses in position. Target is on the move towards the main entrance. Do NOT let that thing past you!"

I dropped my radio and sent dozens of rounds into the UC's path as it scrambled for the exit. Randy had hit the zombie shield with a half-dozen rounds but hadn't slowed the CDC monster's progress towards the main gate. But my strategy seemed to force it to slow and then alter its route, sending the freak for cover under the bleachers.

With no clear shot, I shifted my aim to the moldering corpses left shambling on the fifty-yard-line by their hybrid leader. The plow truck rumbled into the lot, sped into position, and screeched to a halt as the up-armored International pulled sidelong to the emergency exit.

The sweet sound of both M249s purring to life reached me as we shifted our assault into overdrive.

"Randy, keep searching for the smart one. Stone and Andy have the other UCs under control!" I screamed above the chaos of battle.

He responded by shifting his focus to the bleachers, searching for the single most dangerous UC walking the planet.

As the number of targets quickly dwindled, I shot to my feet, my side punishing me for the sudden movement and forcing a yelp before I yelled my intentions to Randy. "I'm going down there. This ends now. Hold your position and cover me."

Randy spun to face me. "Not a chance, Mister Cripple. Take a seat, and you cover *me*."

Ignoring my protest, Randy shouldered his way past me as he barreled into the hall. Indecision gripped me as I vacillated between charging after him and retaking my over-watch position.

The gunfire had trickled to short, controlled bursts indicating the team was mopping up stragglers. I felt a jolt of panic as I raced after Randy. If the team lost track of our primary target, he could easily approach from behind and kill them or escape into the streets and spread the new mutation.

"Stone, Andy, watch your six. We've lost visuals on the hybrid and are no longer in over-watch position. This one is dangerous, boys. And there's no telling what he's capable of."

"Tesha for Otto, I'm at the main gate with a wide view of the east side of the stadium and haven't seen him."

Will's voice crackling from my radio immediately followed Tesha's broadcast. "Otto, I'm on the west side of the stadium and watched him disappear under the bleachers. I haven't seen him since."

"Good news. Hold your positions and radio any updates," I said while gulping air, trying to match Randy's pace. He exploded through large double doors and made a beeline for the field as I dropped further behind. *I'm too old for this...*

My thought shattered as the ground exploded in front of Randy, forcing him to veer hard to his right.

"Who the hell is shooting? You almost killed me!" He barked into his radio as he zigzagged away from the stadium.

Every member of FST1 confirmed they hadn't taken a shot.

"Not good, people. We have another..." The ground exploded in front of me, cutting off my sentence and sending me to the ground seeking cover.

"Otto, move your old ass. We can see you, which means the shooter can too," Stone's voice buzzed from my radio.

He had a point. But my hard landing had knocked the air from my lungs and sent white-hot pain shooting from my side. I laid motionless, hoping the sniper would think he'd scored a kill and move to another target, allowing me to catch my breath. Nothing happened for a ten-count. I rolled to my side and was pelted by flying dirt as the ground just inches from my face erupted.

Rolling hard to my right, I shot to my feet and headed in the same direction as Randy. "Anyone have eyes on the shooter? He's a lousy shot but still dangerous. And he's pissing me off!"

"Otto, this is Will. I hate to ruin your day. That shot came from underneath the bleachers. I caught a muzzle flash and a shadow moving in your direction. I've lost track of him. This SOB has a gun and knows how to use it. RUN!"

I was already running as fast as my old legs allowed. I lost sight of Randy but assumed he had taken up position behind a two-man blocking sled fifty feet away. It wouldn't stop a bullet, but it would make it harder for the shooter to target us.

Three feet from the sled, my head wandered in front of my legs, throwing me off balance. I tumbled to a stop next to Randy, who quickly reached out and dragged me behind the sled.

"You're a hazard, Otto. Seriously, how have you not been eaten by a zombie? It's like you look for ways to make this even harder on yourself."

"Thanks, Randy, I've been asking myself that same question since seventh grade. I really don't have an answer for you."

"Rhetorical question, Otto," Randy said in response to my questioning stare. "I didn't want or expect an answer." He returned to scanning the bleachers through his AR's scope.

Eight minutes later, the team had fallen silent as we scanned the area for our deadly prey. While Will's position offered him the clearest line of sight, the bleachers' design only allowed a few inches of open space between its seats. Coupled with the shadows cast by the mid-day sun and his distance from them, he couldn't pinpoint the monster's location.

The fence stood ten feet tall with privacy slats from top to bottom. The combination made it impossible for us to see anything at ground level.

"Wait a minute," I started, "he had to be able to see us to shoot at us. Scan the upper sections of the bleachers."

Randy shifted his aim up as I radioed my observation to the team.

"Otto, if he's elevated, he's able to climb." Will sounded rattled. We knew what he meant. If he could climb the support beams, he could climb a fence and may have already escaped.

"Well, Randy, you ready to clear a giant football stadium?" I asked while praying he had a better idea.

"No, but it's our only option. The good news is that he's not using a rifle. I didn't see one when I had him lined up, plus I think we'd already be dead. But a bullet's a bullet, and running headlong toward said bullet seems really stupid."

Randy was referring to the wide-open field we needed to cross to reach the bleachers. Not to mention the fact that once we reached them, the only thing separating us from the gun-wielding monster was a chain-link fence.

"Okay then, let's do this before I find a reason not to," I started, then remembered our training. "We zigzag our way to the fence and keep enough distance between us to make him work to kill us both."

We got to our knees and prepared to bolt from cover when Andy's voice crackled from our radios. "I've got a bead on him. I'm going to flush him into the open. Be ready, people."

Randy and I exchanged surprised looks, then broke from cover and ran for our lives toward the fence. I expected to face a wall of bullets, but nothing happened. Not a single round found its way in our direction.

I could hear the team's radio chatter but was too focused on not getting killed to pay attention. I slammed against the fence and, as I caught my breath, the chatter became clear. The monster was on the move with Andy on its tail.

"Randy, we need to get in there."

"No kidding, Otto. Are you ready to climb the fence?" Randy shot back.

The fence! I hadn't thought about what we'd do once we made it here. For some reason, I pictured us simply vaulting over it with guns blazing. Reality hit me with a gut punch; we were fighting a new enemy. The second our heads poked over the fence, that thing would have a clean headshot and end us in seconds.

"Well, now what, Randy?"

He didn't have time to answer as gunfire erupted from behind the fence. "It's close to our position," Randy yelled while searching for cover.

"This was a terrible idea, Randy. Why didn't you talk us out of it? I gave you the chance; now we're going to die. And when they tell our story, it'll start with *they weren't the brightest members of the team.*"

Randy glared at me as he ran past me. I had no idea where he was going, but I wasn't planning to die alone. I turned to follow him when the fence shook violently. I took two steps back and raised my Ruger. With my finger on the trigger, I screamed for Andy to say something. The fence shook more violently in response to my voice.

Indecision gripped me. If Andy were on the other side of the fence, and I pulled the trigger, I'd kill my friend. "Come on, Andy. Answer me."

My answer was thick goo slapping to the ground at my feet. I slowly raised my head and found myself staring into the savage's murderous eyes. The monster sat atop the fence like a gargoyle perched on a medieval church spire, thick drool pouring from his gaping maw. His translucent, blood-spattered skin pulsed with dark bulging veins stretched over sinewy muscles.

"You sneaky little bastard," I said. The beast threw its head back, roaring in triumphant laughter. He had won and was preparing to claim his prize.

It released its grip and sprang into the air; I pulled my Ruger up but knew my effort was futile. A battle cry poured from my lungs as gravity pulled it closer. I locked eyes with my executioner as its body cast my world into shadow. In those eyes, I saw hatred so pure it froze my heart, but not my body. I forced a step back, trying to buy an extra second just as its head evaporated into a pink mist.

My shock gave way to self-preservation, and I scrambled backward to avoid being drenched in the infectious particulate wafting towards me.

Randy's whooping followed the wet slap of the headless beast hitting the ground.

"Did you see that shot? I have to take a picture. Anyone have their phone, or a camera?"

He was running in my direction while patting at his pockets, trying to find his phone. About halfway to my position, he locked me in a hard stare. "I thought you were going to die, Otto."

My head went foggy, and my vision blurred. "I'd like to go home now. I don't want to do this anymore; it's not fun."

I stumbled in Randy's direction as the fence once again shook to life. Pulling my Ruger to my shoulder, I pivoted to face this new threat and found Andy flashing a toothy grin. He placed both hands on top of the fence and vaulted over it, free-falling to the ground.

"What'd I miss?" he said, brushing dirt from his ACUs.

"Only the single greatest shot I've ever made," Randy said, sliding to a stop just short of the blood-soaked earth surrounding the UC's headless body.

"We need to burn the body, and the earth, and our clothes. Then we go home. I want to go home." I hadn't attempted another step; my legs felt like rubber bands, and I really didn't want to fall down again.

Andy stared a question at me while Randy admired his work. "This new variant is more dangerous than any we've seen. Just a drop of it is enough to turn one of us into this." I nodded at the headless carcass. "It's the reason we lost Willis. We can't take the chance of bringing it home. So, we strip to our underwear and burn everything that may have come in contact with this fiend's blood."

Randy finally pulled his attention away from the body. "Otto, I'm not burning my gun or my boots; they're Danners. This," he held out his AR, "is my Daniel Defense. I've had it for years; I love it like it's my child, the son I never had. You can't be serious about burning it... and my boots."

I answered him by tossing my Ruger on top of the UC and peeling off my ACUs. Bright red (and possibly crying), Randy followed suit and tossed his beloved Daniel Defense to the ground and stripped to his tighty-whities. Andy followed suit;

thankfully, he'd left the M249 behind when he flushed the now-headless monster from cover.

I left my gloves on and, before tossing them and my radio onto the pile, radioed Tesha and Will and told them to hold their positions. We would come to them and would ride home in the truck beds.

I attempted to remain as stoic as one can while bouncing around the bed of a dump truck with two other men, wearing only our underwear and nursing a severely blistered face. I focused on the smoke rising from the fire, now distant on the horizon, which was consuming my beloved Ruger.

I sorted through my thoughts. The one at the forefront was how bad the apocalypse hurt; I'm talking physical pain. The books talk about it, but the characters always rebounded, charging courageously back into battle. Not me. I just got hurt and stayed hurt. Every bump, bruise, nick, and cut refused to heal. I wanted a do-over.

Fifteen minutes later, I entered the gates of my community, returning from my last mission as a member of FST1... in my boxers.

Chapter 41 – Luna-tic

It was a beautiful early summer day, a tad warm. I waited behind a line of cars in our grade school's student pickup lane. It felt like a perfectly normal pre-virus day, but the guards perched on the building's roof reminded me of the threat we still lived with.

It was a proper school, not a converted home, or trailer, but a brick and mortar school. We'd reclaimed it from the dead two years earlier and had no shortage of children and teachers to fill it.

I smiled and waved at Maxine (Mac) Divination; she glared back at me from behind the wheel of one of her dad's fuel haulers. Whatever Lisa had told her all those years ago seemed to stick. I still don't know what Lisa said, but at least I remembered Maxine's full name.

Max and his family had joined our community seven years earlier and brought their fuel and knowledge of oil refinement with them. The bombardment at Entry Point One had put them on edge as its intensity grew. But the visit from RAM's military, informing them of their plans to spread the antidote just outside Entry Point One, spurred them to action.

He contacted us via Ham radio and was calling our community home a few short days later. It stunned me to learn how much oil churned beneath Ohio's soil. Our pre-virus output topped five million barrels a year. Within months, Max was producing twenty gallons of petrol a day, more than enough to sustain our community early on.

It only took a year before he decided his family needed more space; actually, we all needed more space. Our community became the beacon of hope we had always known it to be, attracting hundreds of survivors to its promise of a better life.

The push to grow culminated in our ongoing mission, which is now referred to as The Expansion. Our teams move block by city block, house by house, until the area is free of the dead. Then they quickly erect all manner of barricades around the reclaimed land.

Our roadways receive the same treatment as our newly settled communities—cleared of abandoned vehicles and surrounded by cyclone fencing. We've connected every settlement as far south as Olaf's and north to Lake Erie.

The sound of angry little feet slapping the sidewalk broke my thoughts. I turned to look for the little devil those feet belonged to, finding Devon's toothy smile instead.

But I heard the tiny bellow of the angry six-year-old fireball those stomping feet belonged to. "Uncle Otto, you got me in trouble again."

I smiled at Devon, the scar on his cheek reminding me of that fateful day a madman attacked us. "You need a ride home?"

"Thanks, Mister Otto, but I have firefighter training this afternoon. I was escorting Miss Scratchy Bottom to her ride."

"My name is not Miss Scratchy Bottom; it's Luna. And I don't need anyone to walk me anywhere."

Devon and I shared a laugh as he opened the passenger door and helped the tiny version of Lisa into my Yukon. He was growing into a fine young man who had decided to become a firefighter shortly after we'd lost our first house to sparks from a celebratory bonfire. He was still too young to join the Fire Control Team, but we started training our youngsters early these days.

Devon slammed the door and ran towards a crowd of future firefighters awaiting their instructor's arrival.

"My teacher's name isn't Miss McGillicuddy; it's Willis, Addie Willis. I had to stand in the corner during recess because of you." Luna glared at me through her disheveled mop of hair;

her resemblance to her mother was frightening. I had no idea how Dillan survived living with the two of them.

"Nah, she's just testing you. You'll see, when you finally call her Miss Willis, she'll say her name is McGillicuddy and make you stand in the corner again. Safer to stick with what I told you."

"You're crazy, Uncle Otto, just like my mom said."

"But be nice to McGillicuddy. Her brother's a hero."

"I knew it," Luna exclaimed. "Her name IS Willis. We talked about her brother during our history class. Whatever happened to him?"

Funny how seven years later, the mention of my friend still made me mist up. "Well, sweetheart, we don't really know. That stuff he got infected with was wicked. We lost radio contact with him a few weeks after his mission. We had hoped to bring him home; Fort Riley had planned a mission to rescue him. But the last time McMaster talked to him, he noticed a change in Willis, a violent change. It happened two days before the mission was to happen, forcing Fort Riley to scrap their plans. Soon after, he stopped answering our radio calls. Never forget that soldiers like Sergeant Willis made it possible for you and me to live a much safer life. They made the ultimate sacrifice for us. It should serve as a reminder that our freedom comes at the cost of eternal vigilance."

We pulled around Maxine's truck, and she gave a big smiling wave to Luna; she went ice cold when she made eye contact with me.

"You need to tell me what your mom said to Mac."

Luna giggled and kept waving. Just like her mother!

"Speaking of history classes, have they said anything about me? I mean, about FST1?"

Luna went still, but I could see the wheels turning. "Uncle Otto, is it true that we used to have places where people gave you food from a window, and you could eat it anywhere you wanted?"

"Yep, we called it fast food. And I hope it never comes back. That stuff was terrible for you. Except for pizza; we need a good pizza joint. So, still nothing about your old Uncle Otto in history class?"

"Nope, still nothing," she answered while shaking her head vigorously.

I wheeled out of the parking lot and headed for home. "Do you have homework?"

"No, I have shooting practice. Sergeant Major McMaster said he has something special for us today. I like him; he yelled at Sammy for picking on me."

"Why was Sammy picking on you?" I had a feeling I knew the answer.

"He said I looked like a mess. I said he smelled and punched him."

Yep, that's what I figured.

As we drove up to our main gate, Luna was uncharacteristically calm. We waited for the results from the virus test in silence— no fidgeting, no boisterous objections to the mouth-swab, not a peep from her.

After we cleared testing, I asked her, "What's on your mind?"

After a dramatic breath, she said, "Miss McGi... My teacher said that the stories you're telling me are being embel... imbillished. And she told me to tell you to stop it."

"I'm not *embellishing*. I was there, kiddo. All the stories I've told you come straight from the horse's mouth."

Luna's face scrunched up, and she stared at me like I was crazy.

"No, Luna. Horses can't talk. It's just an expression that means the person telling you a story is the person who knows best what happened.

"I'll make you a deal. Ask me about something that happened. Something you can ask someone else to see if I'm telling you the truth."

Her expression told me she already had a story picked out and knew the answer. "Why did my mom punch you in the eye?"

I knew it!

"Well, that's an easy one. I was leading our team home from our first mission, back when MST1 was first formed. Your mom was acting hysterical; I think the pressure was getting to her. I asked her to calm down and told her to have faith in my leadership, that I'd get her home to your dad safe and sound. She snapped and charged me like an unhinged madwoman."

Luna rolled her eyes and put a tiny hand on her forehead. "My teacher was right."

"Okay, okay, she hit me because I called her Wilma."

Laughing her head off, Luna said, "My mom whooped you!"

We pulled up to her house a few seconds later, and I resisted my urge to belittle the child over her statement. And with Dillan standing in his driveway, I couldn't very well make his daughter cry in front of him.

As he walked to retrieve his *bundle of joy*, I leaned in close and said, "Do you know why they named you Luna?" Her attention shifted to me, and she shook her head. "Because you're a Luna-tic. They just shortened it to make it easier to say."

"I don't know what that means, Uncle Otto."

"Ask your mom when she gets home. Don't ask your dad; your mom knows the answer better than anyone. She's very smart."

Dillan leaned through the open window and kissed his daughter. In a flurry of tiny arms and legs, she unbuckled her seatbelt, grabbed her pink backpack, and gave me a peck on the cheek.

"I'll see you tomorrow, Luna."

Without replying, she jumped from the Yukon and scrambled towards the house.

"How's life treating you?" Dillan asked as he watched his wild-child barrel through the door.

"Like it owns the deed to my soul. How about you?"

"Same here." Dillan turned to face me and let his eyes drift to the cane resting between my seat and the center console. "Knee acting up again?"

"Little bit. I need a new one. It could use a stretch. Got a minute to catch up? I don't see you all that much anymore."

Dillan checked his watch. "Yeah, sure. Luna doesn't have to be to firearms training for another hour."

CHAPTER 42 – THOSE NINE WORDS

I grabbed my cane, got out of the Yukon, and rested against its front quarter-panel as Dillan walked around and joined me.

"Speaking of firearms training, when did McMaster take that over?" I asked.

Technically, Sergeant Major McMaster remained attached to Camp Hopkins, but he spent most of his time helping us build a better home for the hundreds of people now living safely behind our walls.

His military connection had been instrumental in our early negotiations for supplies with RAM's military. But that role had diminished as we became more self-reliant.

"About two weeks ago," Dillan responded. "Darline's the mayor; doesn't she tell you anything?"

I chuckled at his comment. We'd elected Darline "mayor" of our small community after Pat passed away in her sleep two years ago. We missed our steely matriarch's commanding presence, but her influence on Darline was clear to this day.

After Pat passed, the community decided it was time to hold elections for our community leaders. We did it by write-in vote, and Darline won in a landslide. She then ordered me to stay out of her business as mayor. Probably the best decision she's made outside of marrying me.

"Well, Dillan, we have an understanding that my input is not welcome. Meaning she tells me nothing, avoiding my opinion."

"Ah, smart lady." Dillan's posture went stiff. "Then you haven't heard about the VIP delegation from Hopkins. They want to talk about trading supplies and go-forward strategies."

"No, they don't. They want Andy. You'd think after seven years of us refusing to turn him over, they'd get the message." I paused, shaking my head in disgust. "They need to stop worrying about Andy and start concentrating on killing zombies. Hell, we've cleared more land around here than they have."

Andy was the only person to survive the virus while remaining an actual human. And the government wanted full access to him in the worst way. We all suspected it was less about a cure and more about replicating his enhanced physical abilities.

Andy's tissue samples and literally hundreds of vials of blood McCune had submitted to RAM were never enough. They wanted to turn him into a lab rat, and we wouldn't let that happen.

To this day, McCune continued to pore over Andy's charts, trying to solve the riddle, but his every attempt had failed. In his years of research, his only accomplishment was temporarily curing cancer and several other nasty diseases. His cancer patient later died of complications from the antidote; actually, all the human test subjects had died. A setback McCune never fully recovered from.

Dillan's voice snapped me back to the conversation. "Do you think they want a cut of our gasoline, or possibly our other outputs?"

My vision went red at the thought. "You mean like a tax? If that's their intent, they better send bachelors to break the news. We will not give up what we've fought for."

Our conversation stopped when FST1's aging Hummer and our two confiscated deuce-and-a-half transports rolled to a stop, blocking the driveway. The smiling faces of FST1's members told me things had gone well.

Lisa was out of her transport before it stopped moving. She glared at me as she walked towards her house. "Did you get my daughter home in one piece?"

"Yes, just like I do every day. You're welcome." My smile always annoyed her, so I made sure it was beaming. "And start checking her schoolwork. I'm not sure she's getting the truth about our history."

It was her turn to smile, and it shed light on my conversation with Luna during our ride home. It wasn't Luna's teacher telling her I was embellishing my stories; it was her mom! Lisa's just plain nasty.

When she disappeared through the front door, I pivoted to Dillan. "You should keep your distance from Lisa tonight, especially after she talks to Luna."

Rubbing his forehead, Dillan asked, "What did you do now, Otto? You're making my life miserable."

Still smiling, I quickly changed the subject and turned to face the team. It felt good to see them standing together. I hadn't interacted with them as much after injuring my knee training new recruits.

It happened six months after our mission at the football field. I'd quit FST1 and moved into an *advisory* role. I finally convinced myself that I was too old, too slow, and tired of being black-and-blue.

In my new role, I helped find and train men and women eager to earn a spot on FST1. I was born to do it. The newbies loved my guidance and appreciated my wealth of knowledge. But a slick spot on a flight of stairs during a house-clearing training session ended my short-lived role.

Nowadays, I manage the gun-cleaning team. The kids on the team adore my stories from my time on the teams. I'm pretty sure they view me as a father figure. Who can blame them?

Randy broke my daydream by slapping my shoulder with his giant paw. "We had a good mission. No shots fired, crude delivered to Max's refinery, and two trucks full of medical supplies."

"And don't forget," Stone interjected, "no one fell down."

"You've been a smartass since we were kids, Stone. I might hate you."

"Nah, you love me, brother; you know you do."

Shaking my head, I made eye contact with Andy. "Look at you! You haven't aged a day. It still creeps me out."

Andy smiled, shrugged his shoulders, and said, "Good genes, Otto."

"Speaking of genes, you need to hide yours in the clinic. The Feds are paying us a visit. No doubt they'll ask about you."

Andy's smile disappeared. "What the actual f.... what don't they understand? When will they be here?"

"Pretty soon. They want a meeting with Darline, council, and McCune," Dillan answered.

Darline stepped from behind my Yukon as Dillan finished speaking. "What about me? Is Otto trash talking again?"

"Hello, your Royal Highness, I wasn't trash talking. In fact, I was just saying how lucky we are to have you as our leader."

Waving a dismissive hand at me, she gave Andy a hug. "I suppose you know about the meeting? They'll be here any minute, so vamoose. We'll let you know when they leave."

Just then, the door to Dillan's house opened, and Lisa joined us with Luna in tow. I waited for her right hand to reach for my throat, but nothing happened. She was actually smiling. Obviously, Luna hadn't asked her about being a lunatic. *Good, let Dillan deal with them later!*

I looked around the group standing in front of me and understood why my dad had always loved the holidays. The people I loved were all here: Darline, Jackson, Dillan, Andy, Tesha, Will, and Randy, maybe even Lisa. I realized at that moment that we had made it, and we were rebuilding our country. The zombie threat would probably be with us forever, but we'd faced it head-on and were no longer merely surviving. We were thriving!

I hadn't realized how much I'd missed them, missed being a part of FST1, until this moment.

"Damn allergies," I said as I wiped at my eyes.

Darline took my hand and snuggled under my arm when Dillan's radio crackled to life, ending the moment.

"Main gate for Dillan."

"Go for Dillan."

"We have a giant motor coach requesting entry for a VIP. I've informed them we are running low on virus tests, and they must submit to a physical bite inspection."

A smile broke on Dillan's face. "So, what's the problem?"

"They're none too pleased about it. A heavily armed man said they're here to help us and shouldn't be asked to follow our protocols."

My left eye twitched at the guard's statement, and I asked Dillan for his radio. Darline tried to stop him; she knew what was happening, but she was too slow.

I had the radio to my mouth an instant later. "Son, hand the radio to the VIP, please."

After a momentary silence, a familiar voice crackled through the radio. "This is President Pace. To whom am I speaking?"

"President? Congrats on your promotion, Pace. Funny, I don't recall an election for a new president. Also, aren't you about a hundred years old? Seriously, why would you even want the job at your age?"

Obviously rattled by my brisk greeting, Pace responded, "I'm sixty-seven. And we don't have the necessary infrastructure to hold national elections. I assure you, once we do, elections will begin again."

"That's odd. Our community managed to hold elections without the *necessary infrastructure*."

"Am I speaking to Otto Hammer? They assured me you were no longer a factor in your community's politics."

"Mister President, I'll always be a factor in my community's wellbeing. Now, I need some clarification. You told our guard you're here to help? Is that correct?"

He tried to respond, but I really didn't want an answer. "Sir, have you ever heard the nine most terrifying words?"

"I'm familiar with them."

"I don't think you are; otherwise, you would have a clearer understanding of their meaning. So, write them down, and refer to them often. The words are as follows: *I'm from the government, and I'm here to help.* Those words signify everything that was and apparently still is wrong with government."

"Otto, I'm not sure what's got you worked up," Pace started, "but I assure you we only want to help your community. Don't say anything to change that."

"Did you just try to blackmail us again?" I interrupted.

"It's extortion, Otto," Darline said while resting her face in her hands.

"Another government official just corrected me. She informed me you're actually trying to extort us. Either way, I'm unhappy, so listen closely: You work for *us*, and we won't allow it to get like it was before. We don't need you; you need us. Hammer, out."

Darline snatched the radio from my hand and moved away while attempting to salvage our relationship with Pace.

"Well, that escalated quickly," Stone started while staring at me wide-eyed. "You know, Otto, we still need them for some stuff."

"Actually, we need them for a lot of stuff," Jackson chirped.

I knew where this was headed and wanted to storm off, but my knee hurt, so I fought back. "No, we don't... name one thing they're doing that we can't do on our own?"

"They're dredging the lake and river of the dead, pulling thousands of them from the water," Stone challenged.

"Don't forget who's guarding and operating the water treatment plants," Jackson said.

"We never ran out of natural gas, even when they thought we would. They kept it flowing," Tesha added.

"Nah, we could've done all that in time. We don't need them... well, maybe a little. But we're doing it, people, we're rebuilding this damn country."

They met my rally cry with stunned silence. So I limped to my Yukon. "I blame Dillan for my behavior; he told me they wanted to tax us. You know how I feel about taxes."

Dillan started to reply, but I cut him off. "You've missed me; you know you have."

I powered up my window, shifted the Yukon into gear, and headed home.

CHAPTER 43 – THAT'S THE STORY

Luna was waiting for me when I arrived to pick her up from school. Her sour expression told me I was in for a long ride home.

She slammed her body into the plush leather seat, buckled in, and crossed her arms.

"You need to shut your door, Luna."

"Oh, whatever!" she snapped and, mustering all the strength in her tiny frame, slammed it shut. Then she returned to her original position and glared out the windshield.

"Long day?"

"You got me in trouble again. I told the teacher that my name is Luna-tic, not Luna. And she should call me by my real name. She didn't believe me, and that made me angry, so I yelled at her. I had to stand in the corner during recess… again."

"You should have asked your mom, not your teacher, Luna. Ask your mom tonight; she'll tell you the truth."

"UNCLE OTTO, Miss Willis told me what lunatic means."

Huh, that didn't go as planned.

She went quiet for a minute, then looked at me as a smile creased her tiny face. "But I got a gold star today."

"Really, did you steal it from Sammy?"

"Ohhhh. You. Make. Me. So. MAD."

"I know, but that's why you love me. So, tell me about your gold star?"

Shaking off her anger, the smile returned to her face. "I turned in my history essay today. Miss Willis told me it was the best she'd ever read."

I became irrationally annoyed by her news. "History, you say. What version of history was your paper about? The authentic version or the one in your books?"

Unfazed, Luna smiled. "The one in my books."

"Oh, for God's sake. That's not accurate at all. Have you been listening to the stories I've told you?" I got so aggravated I had to cut myself off. It's a rare event, but that's how peeved I was.

A tiny giggle pulled my attention to her. I found her holding the paper up, proudly displaying the gold star. "Read it, Uncle Otto."

"I'm driving; I can't read and drive at the same time. Read it to me; I'll tell you where they got it wrong."

Still smiling, Luna said, "Okay, but I'm only going to read the note from my teacher. *Dear Luna, Your essay on the history of our community is the best I've ever read.*"

"That's the same thing you told me a second ago. I'm going to arrange a meeting with your teacher about her lesson plan. She should teach the actual history of your home and how we fought for it."

Hysterical laughter was Luna's response, and it pulled my attention back to her. She held her paper high above her head, waving it back and forth.

I yanked the wheel to the right, steered the Yukon to the berm, and slammed it into Park while snatching the paper from her grubby little hand.

My breath hitched when I read the title: *The History of my Uncle Otto and the Members of FST1*. Kids were reading about me. I mean, us!

Luna leaned in close, and just above a whisper, said, "Thank you, Uncle Otto."

* * * * *

Next From B.D. Lutz

Silenced: Book One of The Consent Of The Governed Series
A political, alternate reality, dystopian thriller

I CAN'T BELIEVE IT; THE SERIES HAS COME TO AN END!

I hope you enjoyed reading it as much as I enjoyed writing it. It'll be hard saying goodbye to some of the characters, especially Otto. And, believe it or not, Lisa. I really enjoyed writing her and Otto's interactions. But I owed it to all of you to keep the story fresh. My fear was that if I kept it going too long, it would become just another zombie book to you, and I really didn't want that to happen.

Thank you for taking this ride with me. I'm eternally grateful to each of you. If you didn't know it, I'll tell you now: You helped me keep a promise I made to myself. Thank you for doing that.

I'd like to thank all of my friends and family for their support. And a special thanks to Heidi, Darline, Charley, Russ, Aundre, and Sean. A quick word about Russ: He is my cousin and the inspiration for the character of the same name in the book. I did, in fact, hit him with a rock. He claims it was in the face, I remember it being his leg. Either way, I hit him with the rock and he deserved it. Love ya, cuz!

Reviews are valuable to independent writers. Please consider leaving yours where you purchased this book.

Feel free to like me on Facebook at B.D. Lutz/Author Page. You'll be the first notified of specials and new releases. You can email me at: CLELUTZ11@gmail.com. I'd love to hear from you.

With all of the strife in our world today, much of it pointed at those of us that still believe in the American Dream, holding on to our ideals is more challenging than we ever imagined, or than it should be. To that I say, remain eternally vigilant to your beliefs, your faith, and yourself!